Tales of Illeross: Gracefully Broken

Ellie Lerum

RED RICHARD ARTS

Contents

To Don and Rita

Thank you for your love and support in this endeavor

CHAPTER ONE

Marin

Marin watched as her friend Rolandus stood before the other Knights of the Long Road. His bow was clutched tightly in his white-knuckled hands.

"You are being promoted to the position of squad leader, Rolandus," a tall redhead said. "You have been serving faithfully, you're receptive to HaMelech, and you have demonstrated your ability for leadership."

"Olare, are you certain?" Rolandus asked.

Olare grinned. "I am. It wasn't a decision I made lightly, nor am I the only one who felt it was time."

A quiet buzz filled the town as they gathered around the knights, hands extended and heads bowed. Marin stared at Rolandus and her brother, her heart sinking to her stomach.

It was time for Apple Ridge, their home, to send a relief group to one of the more dangerous parts of the country. Bleak Hollow needed fresh support to escort travelers through the forest and past the chittering demons that lived there. This month, Olare was leading a squad and Rolandus was going with him.

The hunched priest of HaMelech made his way to the 16 selected to serve, his hand trembling as he rested it on Rolandus' arm. In a creaking voice, he said, "HaMelech keep you, young Rolandus..." He trailed off, searching the crowd, before his eyes rested on Marin. "Miss Lott, join the other Doves as we pray."

Marin blinked before she approached.

This was reserved for higher-sanctioned healers, not one completing training. She rested her hand on Rolandus' back and then her head against his temple, sighing. Another month would pass before she could see him again, before she could rest beneath the apple trees alongside him and watch the snow fall from rooftops.

"HaMelech, thank You for being with us today and thank You for creating men and women who are willing to serve on the battlefield in Your name. We ask that You bless Master Rolandus with your supernatural wisdom as he steps into a new position and that You grant him success as he continues to listen to your Breath." The priest paused for a moment as though he was listening to something. Then he murmured, "May Your will supersede our own, as You are perfect and your will is, too."

As they prayed, Marin whispered, "May HaMelech guide you and protect you... all of you... and may He bring you back to me."

Marin realized she was crying when the priest said the final words of the prayer. Rolandus wiped her face. "It'll be okay, remember? Like you've said before: HaMelech will hold me."

She nodded at him, offered a shaking smile, and then flung her arms around him. Rolandus held her before they pulled away and Olare stepped to her.

As he hugged her, Marin sighed. "Promise me you'll come back... and promise me that you'll bring Rolandus home, too."

"I promise," Olare said. They watched as the young archer fastened his bow to his back and swung onto a large ram. "He'll be fine, Marin."

"I know, but..." Marin trailed off.

"He's dear to you, I know," Olare murmured. He chuckled. "I know that you care about him, especially after everything we've been through. HaMelech sent him exactly to where he needed to be."

Marin nodded again before she whispered, "Promise me that you'll keep an eye on him and bring him home, please."

"I will."

Their conversation ended as others from Apple Ridge flitted around the Knights of the Long Road. Marin approached Rolandus' war ram again, finding that he was already waiting for her to say a final goodbye. She brushed a couple of stray dreadlocks from his face as he leaned. "Be careful. If you must wear your mantel, do so: HaMelech blessed you with it, so please use those gifts He gave you. I'll be praying for you and the company while you're gone."

Rolandus smiled and pressed his forehead to her own. "I will, Marin. I won't lie, the thought of facing chitters makes me... anxious."

"HaMelech will guide your bow, Rolandus, you know that," Marin murmured. "HaMelech is so much mightier than a hoard of chitters, and He will watch you. He's done this since you were first brought here, and He continues to do so as you work with the sheepdogs."

They were unable to say much more before the company rode away, leaving Marin in a cloud of dust as she watched them go.

It took a moment for her to leave the town center and then go to the apple tree where she and Rolandus would often meet. Then, she pulled a well-worn book from her bag.

In her mind's eye, she could see HaMelech's three-peaked mountain over a band of thorns. It was a symbol that she had become familiar with since joining the Dove healers. Peace flooded over her and she murmured, "It's a beautiful day that You've blessed me with. I'm glad to be able to spend it with You, and that You blessed me with such a beautiful friendship with Rolandus. Please... keep them all safe while they are gone."

There was the slightest prickle of tears in her eyes as she opened them, staring at the leaves above her. She was fortunate that Rolandus was sent before her father passed. He reminded her of HaMelech's grace and was a listening ear while Olare was away.

The woman remained under the tree for fifteen minutes before she stood and started into town.

Most people were either busy working or were in their homes. The streets were quiet, as was the temple, except for the gentle murmur of conversations among the Dove healers.

After signing the logbook, Marin found her mentor, Sister Iren. The older Dove had been kind enough to take Marin under her guidance years ago. She continued to show Marin the best ways to bandage wounds, help laboring women, and serve HaMelech throughout the day.

Marin watched as Iren ground a handful of herbs with a pestle, enjoying the spice that filled the air as Iren explained the need to make the herbs as powdered as possible. It was the most interesting thing that happened that day.

Her walk to the temple was quiet the next morning. It was still dark, before dawn, and most everyone was still sleeping. Marin pulled her shawl around her shoulders, listening to the birds in the trees and the war rams in the nearby stables.

As she entered the temple, scanning the white stone walls, Marin found that she wasn't the only one there.

Sister Iren was already before the altar, praying with her eyes closed. Marin joined her mentor, kneeling before the wooden pulpit, and then closed her eyes.

Eventually, her mentor murmured, "It is going to be a long day, Marin."

She stood. "Your learning is beginning to slow down. On one hand, it means that you are nearly ready to take on the duties and responsibilities of a fully fledged Dove. On the other, your skills must be perfected as it is now the time to ensure that you have what it takes to enter the calling."

"Of course," Marin said. "I'm excited to see what HaMelech has in store. I know this is the path I'm being called to."

Iren smiled at her. "I know, Marin. You've blossomed into quite the young woman and a well-versed healer. There is always room to improve, just as in every aspect of life, but I know that you will reach those marks before you know it. HaMelech has a beautiful plan for you."

Pride filled the younger redhead and she smiled, looking straight ahead. She and Iren commenced their rounds, during which Iren mostly stood back, observing.

Marin glanced back at Iren for approval as she finished checking over a little boy's arm. "That's it. I've applied a yarrow poultice to help with inflammation, I've written that I'd like a comfrey tincture once the cut is healed, and I've bandaged it. There's no fever, so infection hasn't set in and shouldn't. Is there anything else?"

Her mentor inspected the bandage, finally nodding. "Not until we check it again. We can send the comfrey home with his mother; she'll know what to do with it and when it may be applied. Well done, Marin."

Two weeks after the knights' departure, Marin was engrossed in a ledger when footsteps reverberated in the hallway behind her. She glanced back to see it was Iren. "Marin, there's a small group leaving tomorrow morning with comforts from home and a resupply for our knights in Bleak Hollow. Would you like to go and see them?"

"Of course! It would be nice to see them. I know that it hasn't been long, but if it'll help bolster their spirits I would love to," Marin said.

Before she knew it, she was in a wagon lurching down the well-worn road to Bleak Hollow. It took a week for them to arrive at Last Hope. The last day included an escort by the Bleak Hollow Brigade as they moved through the cursed forest.

Marin stared at the woods around them and then glanced at one of the escorting knights. "Where are the Apple Ridge troops? I thought we might have been escorted by them to Last Hope."

The knight shook her head. "No, Captain Olare and two of his squads are coming back from Garren's Stand. With any luck, we'll meet them in Last Hope or beat them there." She shouldered her axe. "The other two squads are already in the fortress."

Marin nodded, catching sight of the large stone keep that towered above the trees in the distance. As they got closer, she studied the walls and the raging winter river that surrounded it. Large chunks of ice flowed past the drawbridge and massive gate that separated the forest from the fort inside. It was imposing even after they passed through.

As the wagons drew to a halt, Marin was helped down. Then, she and the other five Doves began to unpack the supplies they had brought. The redhead looked around as she passed packages around, trying to catch a glimpse of either Olare or Rolandus.

Last Hope was a rather cramped fort. To the west, a row of stone buildings were attached to the fortress wall, one of which predominately displaying the symbol of HaMelech. On the eastern wall, a smaller set of buildings with the symbol of Solaris on banners took up that space. A courtyard ran through the center, almost a silent declaration of the feud that had been going since before the dawn of time. As the sun made its rapid approach to the horizon, Marin's heart began to sink.

Just as she was about to give up looking for the two men, a sudden clamor of shouting and hoofs on cobblestone rang through the square. Marin turned to see a massive tide of people- Knights, mechanical Shepherd suits, Doves, Solari guards, and caravaning individuals-crash through the gate. Most of them seemed alright, though panic was stark on their face as Solari and Kingsmen alike ran towards them.

Olare was in the back of the group, mounted atop his war ram. Another ram was tethered to his saddle and, slumped in front of him, was Rolandus.

Marin raced towards them, doing her best to swim through the crowd. As she grew closer, she realized that many in this group were covered in oozing black injuries. Some were on stretchers, some were on rams or horses, and all seemed stunned.

She grabbed the reins of Olare's ram, who shot back before it recognized her. Olare's hand flew to his sword. "Release... Marin! What are you doing here?"

"Marin?" Rolandus croaked.

He lifted his head, a weak smile on his face, before he grimaced and slouched again. Olare muttered under his breath. "Help me get him down... summon our other Doves! We've got injured!"

Marin took Rolandus' arms and helped him from the ram as more healers pooled around them. It was a deafening roar as Rolandus leaned into her, holding onto his side as she looked at Olare. "What happened?"

"Chitter ambush. They had an accursed chitter Champion leading... Oi!" Olare snapped.

Marin jumped and watched as her brother drew his sword. He pointed its glowing blade at an imposing figure in white armor and cloak, his face completely hidden by a black void under his cowl.

It was a Solari inquisitor, his naked blade wreathed in flames as a stark contrast to the soft light that emitted from Olare's.

"Put her down, now!" Olare barked.

Marin followed his gaze to the inquisitor's left hand. He had a woman by the hair as she whimpered, begging him to release her.

Marin could see there was a nasty bite on her shoulder that oozed black bile, huge compared to the numerous small wounds that covered the rest of her exposed skin.

"She is infected beyond what even your witches can heal." The inquisitor gestured to the injured around them. "We are only protected from those demons infiltrating the fort by Solaris' divine province." He then looked at the rapidly setting sun, which had already dropped below the outer wall and plunged the courtyard into shadow, "Provence that is rapidly diminishing."

Marin's attention was drawn back to Rolandus as he groaned, trying to sit up. He clung to his bow and she shushed him. "Lie down... it's alright."

"No... they need me..." Rolandus stared at her, his eyes exhausted, before the strength in his body left him and he collapsed in Marin's arms again.

Marin held him tighter, opening her mouth to argue before she swallowed.

The inquisitor had been joined by two more, as well as a dozen guards wearing the livery of Garren's Stand, who stood across from the Knights of the Long Road in a silent line. While only two blades were drawn, the tension in the air was palpable.

"Move the injured to the chapel, civilians first!" Olare barked. With a flurry of activity around the two lines of soldiers, every abled-bodied man and woman began to usher the wounded from the streets.

"You are a fool, heretic. You should let us cut out the rot while there is still light," the inquisitor said.

Olare glanced at him, set his jaw, and straightened up. "You know the rules of the treaty. As long as the sun is shining, you are not to harm the injured." He lowered his voice ever so slightly. "Be aware that if you try to cull one of my men, even after the sun sets, I will take it as unprovoked aggression."

The inquisitor sighed and then looked at the tallest tower. Marin followed his gaze to see that the shadows had already consumed most of it. He was silent for a moment before he let his sword hang by his side. "Very well, but you had better hurry."

"Give me the woman."

"There is nothing in the treaty that prevents me from detaining an injured civilian so long as she comes to no harm before the sun sets." The inquisitor gave a quick gesture and the guards moved forward in an attempt to secure some of the wounded. The line of knights blocked their attempts, but none dared draw their weapon.

The last light was punctuated by a gurgling hiss and the smell of burnt flesh. Marin, against her best attempts, gave a startled cry as the inquisitor severed the injured woman's body from her head. He pointed his blade at Olare. "Stand aside, heretics. You impede the cleansing."

Olare gave a peevish smile, leaning in to murmur, "There is nothing in the treaty preventing us from just standing here."

The inquisitor clenched his sword as the last of the civilians were rushed into the chapel. As soon as they were, Olare helped Marin stand Rolandus and they, and the other injured knights, followed behind.

The small chapel was packed to bursting. People laid both atop and below the rows of wooden pews as doves rushed about. Scattered amongst them were knights, their swords drawn and the golden edges of their weapons gently lighting the room.

"What happened, Olare?" Marin looked at him as she wiped Rolandus' wounds. Her friend writhed under her hand, and she gently hushed him, doing her best to wrap the injuries tightly to stop any more bleeding.

Olare sighed, his eyes never stopping their scan of the room. "Like I said before, we were attacked by a chitter champion. Usually, those monsters are uncoordinated and simply throw themselves into battle with little regard. Sometimes, though, there is a smart one... and this time, it had managed to rally a considerable horde. A wave crashed into the front lines and we were doing well enough before some of the spooked green soldiers in the back rushed forward to help. That was when it showed up.

"We call it Skull-Stealer. It's a chitter warrior that wears a human skull as a helmet and who wields a cleaver forged in darkness. It and its vanguard attacked the back of the convoy." Olare was silent for a long moment. Finally, he whispered, "Rolandus and his squad fought valiantly, but we didn't drive them off without casualty. Gregory, the potter's son from down the road, is among the fallen. I managed to arrive in time to avenge him and prevent one of those thrice-cursed monsters from running off with his head but..." he shook his head, "I managed to take their champion out of the fight, but it was too late at that point..."

Marin took his hand. "You were able to at least get everyone back."

"Everyone living. We had to run before we could collect the fallen. Tomorrow, at first light, I will be taking a small group to retrieve the bodies." Olare looked away from her. "Maybe HaMelech-"

"HaMelech didn't do this to you, Olare, and I know that He doesn't like to see His children hurting like this..." Marin trailed off, looking at Rolandus as he lay in her arms. "He knows what we need. It's terrifying to say, but I am afraid that... He isn't currently listening. I don't want to think that, but I'm so frightened. This is a new experience and with Rolandus..."

"You love him, don't you Marin?" Olare asked, tilting his head. He stared at his sister, his green eyes intense. "I figured that you do... given the letters you sent me years ago that gushed about him and the time you spend with him now."

Marin blinked, tears beginning to fill her eyes again. She nodded, laid Rolandus down, and then took his hands in her own. "I do, and I don't want to lose him. Not now, not anytime soon. I know HaMelech will hold him when the time comes but... right now, I want to be the one to hold him."

Olare smiled a little more. "He's lucky to have you in his life. We both are. I know he cares for you, too; he talks about you a lot and is gentle with you. You're good for him. Now... now he needs you more than ever." He shifted before reaching towards the wall where Rolandus' old bow leaned.

Attached to the bow was a bundle of feathers, which Olare removed and handed to Marin. "Here, put his mantle on him. It'll be cold soon, and this will provide extra warmth and comfort."

Marin took the bundle and tied it to his wrist.

It was almost mesmerizing to watch as the dusky brown feathers covered his entire body. A beak formed and soon a falcon hybrid lay on the bed, sleeping where Rolandus once was.

She stroked his feathers and then began to pray. "HaMelech... I don't know what to do, all I know is that I'm scared, I'm unsure... and I need help." The sudden feeling of tears welling into her eyes made her press her face to Rolandus' temple, beginning to cry. "Please... I need help. We... we need help. I can't do this on my own.

"Rolandus needs Your hand of healing- he needs You to act as I cannot do anything. I have no control, I do not know, and..." she trailed off, "and I don't want to lose him."

She prayed over him for what felt like hours, whispering prayers and petitions to HaMelech. About halfway through her prayer, she realized that a light golden sheen had begun to cover her friend as she spoke.

Towards dawn, Rolandus startled from his sleep again. This time, he knocked heads with Marin as he looked around. "There... there!" Marin followed his gaze to see the shadows were beginning to form creatures in them. Olare stood from the wall, pulling his sword, as a long-legged rabbit stepped out. Its fangs dripped with the same black ooze that seeped from Rolandus' side and, without a sound, it lunged. Olare cut it down with a single swing of his blade as others in the room began to cry out. Within a handful of moments, the various beasts that appeared from the shadows as the injured writhed in pain or panic were ended by the hardlight weapons, and Marin went back to praying for Rolandus.

This time, she held both of his hands. "Rolandus, can you hear me?" He nodded weakly and she whispered, "Good... HaM-elech is here, He is keeping you. It's okay, you're going to be okay."

She brushed some of his hair from his face, falling back to her prayer before a hand rested on her shoulder. "We're going to prepare the injured to move to Godrick's Rest."

Marin looked at the other Dove, frowning until the man continued, "They have more experience with chittering madness than we do here. No one recovers from the wounds left by those demons while inside these woods, and the Doves in Godrick's Rest can actually treat the madness. They'll take good care of your friend in your stead."

"In my stead? No, I'm going with Rolandus," Marin said. She turned to face him. "I'm not letting him go alone, even with others to help him: I need to remain with him. He doesn't know any of the Doves who will be serving him, the very least I can do is be someone of familiarity and comfort."

It took a moment before the man nodded. "If that is what you wish to do, be ready to leave within the hour. If you aren't with the wagon by the time we move, we will not wait for you."

The hour flew by quicker than Marin had realized and, as it did, she found herself giving Olare a tight hug before she followed the small caravan of injured out of the gates and into Bleak Hollow once more.

CHAPTER TWO

Godrick's Rest

The day-long journey to Godrick's Rest was stifling between trying to calm the injured and a constant threat of chitters.

A majority of the wounded were able to sit up despite their injuries. They were covered in bandages and jumped at the shadows they passed, but they were doing alright. Rolandus seemed to be doing the worst: blood and black ooze seeped through the bandages that crisscrossed over his body and he shivered most moments.

They rolled into Godrick's Rest near the evening meal. Marin helped Doves from both the caravan and the town remove injured from the wagon. Rolandus was brought in on a stretcher into the temple, which was quiet and sterile.

Each person lay on a bed as they waited for inspection. Marin sat beside Rolandus, holding his hand and stroking his hair again. He shifted, whimpering, before he pressed his face to her hand. Marin sighed and kissed his forehead.

As she focused on Rolandus, a woman who looked to be close to 70 hobbled into the infirmary. She tapped her cane on the floor as she walked, her sightless gray eyes focused ahead of her. The woman made her way to them, where she sat beside Marin and found Rolandus' hand.

Marin shifted. "Excuse me?"

"Oh, I'm sorry dear. I didn't realize someone was with this young man," the old woman whispered. She looked towards Marin, her face gentle. "I don't recognize your voice, you must be new to Godrick's Rest. You came with him, didn't you?"

"I... did." Marin watched the woman as she held Rolandus' hand and began to pray. Finally, she asked, "Who are you?"

"Me? My name is Leticia, but you can call me Grandma Letty, dear one. What's your name, and who is your friend?"

"Marin, and this is Rolandus. Are you a Dove, too?"

Grandma Letty paused. "No, but I'm here to help regardless." She smiled towards Marin, found her leg to give it a comforting pat, and turned back to Rolandus.

Letty's presence had a familiar and comforting quality to it. Marin felt safe beside her and, as she caught some of Letty's quiet words, she knew that Rolandus was, too. They sat together for fifteen minutes before a hushed, "Mom, what are you doing here?" interrupted them.

Marin turned to see a young woman hurrying towards them. "Madame Sinmi is coming back to inspect the new arrivals, and if she catches you in here-"

"Marin, this is my daughter Penny. Penny, this is Marin: she came with young Master Rolandus." Letty looked towards where her daughter stood. "Madame Sinmi has caught me in this temple far more times than you know. I am obedient to the will of our God, and I am willing to take beratement from others as I do so."

"Who's Madame Sinmi?" Marin asked.

Before Penny or Letty could answer, a door across the hall opened and a severe-looking woman stepped out. As she looked around the injured who were lining the walls, she paused as she saw Rolandus. Her gaze continued to sweep the room and she began to bark orders, all the while hurrying towards them.

Penny stood up straight. "Madame Sinmi-"

"How many times have I told you to keep your mother out of my temple?" Sinmi snapped. "And you, Letty, know that you are not welcome here!"

"I am doing nothing of harm, Sinmi, merely praying over injured as I know how," Letty answered. She stood, almost sheltering Marin from Sinmi's sight. "On that note, I want to extend-"

"You will do nothing but leave, or I will have a knight remove you." Sinmi paused, seeing Marin from behind the old woman, and then frowned. As soon as her gaze moved from her to Rolandus, the frown turned to concern. "Penny, call two knights. He needs to be moved away from the others."

"Why?" Marin asked.

All three women looked at her and she shifted. "Why do we need to remove him? He isn't contagious- if he was, I would be ill now as well."

"That is none of your concern, young lady! Your ignorance shows how little you know about this issue. It's time for you to leave the temple. Visiting hours are now closed."

Marin stared at Sinmi as Penny hurried off to do as she was told, finally shaking her head. "I'm not leaving his side."

"And I'm not allowing you to join him," Sinmi replied. "Go with Letty and you may return after the surgery-"

"What surgery?"

Sinmi frowned. "He is going in for an amputation. It's best to remove the infected limb before it spreads to the rest of his body. Now, it's time for you to leave-"

"I'm not leaving, especially when the only thing you deem 'treatment' is amputation!" Marin exclaimed. She sat down, her eyes narrow.

"Until HaMelech releases me from Rolandus' side, I will remain with him."

She stared at the older woman, her chest heaving, before a gentle hand rested on her arm. Letty looked towards her. "Marin, it will be okay."

Marin looked at Letty before the elderly woman began to move from the temple, leaving them. As she did, Penny returned with two Knights of the Long Road. "Let's find you a place to stay overnight, miss-"

"I'm not leaving," Marin repeated.

One of the knights lifted Rolandus' arm over his shoulder to stand him upright. The other knight took Marin's hand and made her stand as well. "Come on, miss, he'll be in better hands here."

Marin stared at the four. "I serve the One True King as a Dove apprentice. Rolandus is my friend, and I love him dearly: I will not let him go through this alone, not when he knows only me here and most certainly not when the only thing that you're willing to do to help him is to remove..."

Simni stared at her before Penny murmured, "Perhaps she can stay with him before the surgery? That couldn't possibly hurt, could it?"

"If he manifests any chitters, it could," Simni argued back. The head Dove sighed. "I will, however, make an exception this one time. Make her sign some waivers, and then she may join him. And you-" she looked at Marin, "you are only an apprentice Dove, and have no idea about what plagues this land. You are inferior in your knowledge and must submit to the authorities over you. The moment he is done with surgery, you are to inform me of who your mentor is and I will speak to them about this... outburst."

With that, she turned on her heel and left. Marin stared at Penny. "Thank you... thank you so much."

Penny offered a little smile in return before she and the knights led Marin and Rolandus down a hallway. Then, they laid Rolandus in a small room atop a cot. Marin sat beside his bed, staring at the plain, cold stone walls around her. "Is this where you keep everyone ready for surgery?"

"... just those with severe chittering madness," Penny murmured. "He'll sleep the entire time he's in here and wake up in a nice bed once it's over."

She started to the door and then paused. "Marin, you realize that the amputation isn't just his arm... right? His legs are covered in bites, too."

Marin shook her head. "There must be another way."

Penny offered a sad smile and left without a word. The knight who had helped Rolandus in stepped out as well, leaving Marin, Rolandus, and the knight who had led her in. They stayed silent for several minutes before Rolandus began to whimper and shift. Marin shifted to kneel beside him, taking one of his hands in her own. "It's okay, Rolandus. HaMelech has you." She squeezed her eyes closed, trying not to cry, and began to pray. "HaMelech, you are so much mightier than any of us on this planet. Thank you for your mercies-"

"You're wasting your breath," the knight said.

Marin glanced at him out of the corner of her eye and went back to prayer only to be interrupted again. She sighed, looked at the ceiling, and then at the knight. "Look, I get that you're supposed to be here to keep things from going wrong but... please, I want to spend this time in prayer with him."

The knight pushed off of the wall. He studied Rolandus for a moment before he said, "They'll be taking both legs and at least one of his arms. You know that he won't be able to do anything once they do, right? If he was serving as a knight, he's going to be pulled from duty and he'll be useless." He crouched beside Marin. "It's sweet that you're trying to convince HaMelech to do something, but as I've seen many cases like this... you're better off letting him enter his new life without attachment."

Marin frowned and the knight murmured, "You've been through a lot- he won't be able to help you from here on. He'll be staying here, watched the rest of his life... he won't be able to do anything for you."

"I am not leaving his side."

The knight watched her, finally smiling. He reached out and tucked a piece of hair behind Marin's ear. "Perhaps I could convince you otherwise? You have so much to look forward to in life... you shouldn't waste your time with him, especially when I can give you everything you want."

He moved his hand from her hair and ran it down her cheek. "Think about it: a knight, willing to take you into his home, place you on a pedestal... rather than staying beside a cripple your entire life."

Marin blinked and then struck his hand away. "Get away from me, I want nothing from you."

"You don't know what you want," he replied."You're scared, delusional, and are confused about what's going on." He grabbed her arm and Marin began to struggle. "Don't fight it, sweetheart, it'll be less pleasant for both of us. Just give in and let me soothe your nerves-"

"Let go!"

As Marin struggled, she suddenly became aware of three things. The first was that the knight was fumbling with his belt. The second was that Rolandus was beginning to writhe on the bed. On the other side of the bed, beginning to form from shadows, was the third. A lithe chitter form was pulling itself from the darkness and, in its hand, a dagger darker than obsidian glinted in the weak light.

The woman froze. She could see a cold, calculated intelligence in this demon rather than the seemingly mindless fury that its brethren seemed to have and, in an instant, the room was filled with its horrid cackling. The knight turned as soon as it began to laugh, his pants half down his legs, and released Marin. He struggled with his sword, pulling it just in time to deflect the dagger that had been thrown at him. With the blade reforming in its hand again, the chitter jumped over the bed and crashed into a tussle. The two combatants rolled on the floor as the chitter bit and brandished its weapon and the knight tried to defend himself.

Wasting no time, Marin flung herself at Rolandus. As soon as she began to shake him, his eyes opened and he looked around in panic. "Where-"

"Get up, we have to go, now!" Marin said. She hurried him to his feet, struggling under his weight as she managed to get them to the door. By this point, the chitter in the room had been subdued and the knight was trying to get his pants back up.

"Stop! Get back here!"

"Run, Rolandus!" Marin begged, "Please, we need to run!"

Her friend made a sound of pain but forced himself harder as Marin got them from the room and into the hallway. The added panic of their escape fueled more chaos. Around them, the shadows swirled and manifested eyes and dangerous fangs. Each branched off and laughed as the knight shouted for help.

A handful of the chitters pulled themselves from the shadows and ran after Marin and Rolandus as they fled the temple, nipping at their heels before they were distracted by the unsuspecting knights and Doves that ran towards them to figure out what was wrong.

Marin stumbled twice during their run. She lost her shoe during the first trip, and the second time it was due to a chitter sinking its teeth into her leg.

Despite Rolandus' injury and panic, the moment Marin cried out he acted. His hand flashed to the once forgotten hunting knife Marin carried on her hip and he stabbed the creature.

Marin struggled to her feet and they burst out of the temple. They ran until her lungs burned, and even then, they only stopped when she realized that Rolandus was weeping. She sat him down and clung to him. "Rolandus, Rolandus, I'm so sorry... It burns, I know it burns, I'm sorry..."

He held onto her and Marin stroked his hair, trying not to sob as well. The bite on her leg stung, but she knew it was mild compared to what Rolandus was going through. She stared at the sky. "HaMelech... please, help us. I don't know what to do... We... we need to go, but there isn't anywhere to go. Send someone, anyone..." she trailed off and hung her head.

Rolandus' grip tightened and he managed, "Marin, it'll be okay."

"It won't! We don't have a place to go, and... and you're injured and..." Marin stared at her friend, searching his face. His eyes were exhausted, especially when he donned his mantle in an attempt to keep them warm. He pulled her close and Marin pressed her face to his chest. "I'm so sorry, Rolandus... I'm supposed to be a Dove healer, and instead, I removed us from the temple, and... and left a mess... and you...."

Rolandus shook his head. "I'll... I'll be okay. Just rest, you were bitten too."

Marin moved her skirt to inspect the injury, too tired to care about the black venom that dripped from the punctures. She swallowed and rested her head on Rolandus' chest again. "It's okay, it isn't bad."

They sat as shouts echoed from the direction of the temple. Marin could hear Sinmi demanding that they be found, other voices were shouting about the chitters that had manifested, and still more were knights calling for extra support in checking over wounded.

The young healer finally sniffled, "I'm sorry I caused this... HaMelech, I'm sorry that I caused this issue, and the chitters and... please, forgive me." Rolandus held her tighter and pressed his beak into her hair.

A quiet tapping made Marin lift her head, her body stiff. She wasn't sure how long they had been sleeping, but she did know that they had been kept safe from unwelcome eyes. She looked around before seeing a hunched figure approaching with a cane. As the figure approached, Marin found that it was Letty. "Grandma Letty?"

"There you are! Stand up, let's get you inside," Letty said. She found Marin's hand to help her stand and then paused as Marin burst into tears. "What's wrong?"

"I'm so sorry!" Marin managed. "I... I didn't mean to make chitters appear, or to hurt Rolandus anymore, and... and I know it's my fault!"

"Oh, sweet child..." Letty held Marin near as the girl sobbed. "Alright, your pity party isn't going to solve anything. Let's get you and young Master Rolandus somewhere you can rest, and we can figure out the next steps then, okay? Come along and pay no mind to the shadows- my friend will not let them enter my home."

Marin nodded, wiped her eyes, and crouched beside Rolandus. The cote was still sleeping, covered in feathers, and he opened one eye as she shook him. "We need to get going. Someone is here to shelter us for the next while, alright?"

Rolandus managed to stand and then fell into her arms. "I don't know if I can go very far."

"It isn't far, child," Letty said.

If Marin weren't in pain, or worried for Rolandus, she would have laughed at how close they had been all along: if they had gone no more than 50 feet further into the little hamlet, they would have been on Letty's doorstep.

Instead, she was silent as they limped Rolandus to a bedroom and laid him down. The shadows around them swirled, threatening to become the demonic creatures that had caused their pain, but Marin did her best to focus on Rolandus. He groaned, his hand searching for Marin's, and he clung to it as fear and agony washed over his face. Marin stroked his hair. "I don't know what to do. I don't know what you need..."

"Take a breath, Marin," Letty said. "I am going to fetch him some herbs, I want you to talk to him and make him comfortable."

Comfortable? Marin's voice trembled as she whispered, "We should be safe here."

He squeezed his eyes closed with a nod and held onto her hand. Marin tightened her grip on his hand before pressing her forehead against his. In the silence of the room, she began to pray again, "HaMelech, thank you for all you have done: you have kept us safe despite the monsters that hide in the shadows, and you brought me and Rolandus together despite all that's happened. You are mighty, and You are there to protect your children regardless what happens, help me, please... I... I am so sorry I caused so many people pain, and that I made such a mess. I didn't mean to, and..." she trailed off, "I don't know what I'm doing."

Rolandus shifted against her, squeezing her hand, before he sighed, "Marin, you need to rest."

"I need to tend to you first."

"You can't do anything if you are doing poorly as well," he said. "I will be alright until dawn."

Marin nodded. Rolandus fell asleep after a few minutes, and then Letty entered the room again. "Alright, dear, what's happened to you?"

"I was bitten. Chitters began to form in the temple and as I ran." Marin quietly lifted her skirt to show the bite. Black ichor and pus seeped from the puncture marks even after her brief rest. She stared at it. "It... looks horrible."

"Grit your teeth then." Letty crouched beside the bed with a bowl of steaming water. On the surface was a handful of lavender petals and, taking a majority of the space, a light-yellow flower with orange spots. It smelled comforting in a strange way, akin to that of a relaxing bath or a walk in the field, as a strange scent of cinnamon wafted from the mixture. Letty dipped a cloth into the water and reached toward Marin's leg when the redhead shifted away.

"Can you help Rolandus, first?"

Letty looked at her. "No, Marin. Master Rolandus will be okay until you are tended to. We need to do far more work on him if he is manifesting chitters, the poor thing. Brace yourself, the Valri will help with your bites, but it will sting." Marin bit her tongue as Letty applied the hot water to her injury, nearly crying out as Letty then pressed on the inflamed area.

It oozed puss and ichor, burning with each moment. Letty finally murmured, "I can only imagine how poorly tended to young Master Rolandus' injuries are. Cleaning must be done daily to remove the venom, and if it isn't, it'll get just as bad as this. How long has he been dealing with his wounds?"

"We left Last Hope nearly two days ago," Marin mumbled. She balled her fist around the blanket underhand. "I tried washing his wounds when he first received them, and shortly before we left, but they haven't been since we arrived here. I should have done something, but instead, I ran."

"Marin, focus," Letty said back. She looked up at Marin, her sightless gray eyes gentle, "What happened is now in the past, it is time to focus on the now. Rolandus needs you to focus on him, and I need you to focus as well. Let me finish cleaning your bite and then we will tend to your friend. Alright?"

Marin nodded, silent as Letty continued to clean her leg. After 20 minutes, Letty left. She returned with fresh, steaming water and herbs, this time carrying a small bottle and dropper, "Start with the bandages on his chest."

As soon as Marin uncovered the first wound, she nearly vomited.

Like her leg, the wound looked infected. It was red, hot to the touch, and oozed. Around the gash were black tendrils that seemed to snake under his skin, surrounding where his heart would be and traveling toward his neck. Marin stared at him, her fingers beginning to tremble.

Letty didn't speak as she found Marin's hand and pressed the cloth to it. "It is time to clean it, and we will open the blinds come daybreak. What is it doing?"

"... It is consuming him," Marin whispered.

The old woman placed the hot water on the bedside table and pulled out the dropper. "I have a tincture I want him to take and I will help you after I do so. It'll take two hands if it's that bad."

Marin nodded, beginning to wipe at the ichor. The first touch of the cloth made Rolandus convulse, his eyes wide as he cried out in pain. Marin kept the cloth on his chest, one hand on his cheek. "Rolandus, please calm down! It's only me, it's alright."

He stared at her, trembling, and then nodded. Marin stroked his cheek with her thumb and began to wash his wounds again. Letty applied the tincture under Rolandus' tongue, murmuring in an unknown language. Rolandus closed his eyes once more, breathing as deeply as he could despite the pain.

Marin shifted. "There are so many bites... will he be able to recover from the chittering madness? You said that it's bad if he's making chitters appear, how does that happen? Will he do it again?"

Letty shook her head. "He doesn't have chittering madness, not yet. He's declining toward it, but this is only chittering sickness. Unfortunately, it can, and will, get worse if we don't tend to it."

Marin blinked, "Is there anything to do to cure it? I've been praying but that hasn't... that hasn't done anything."

"Sh, calm down," Letty murmured. "He isn't that far gone, there's always hope for recovery. I've taken the time to listen to the Breath and learn how to tend to those with the illness. That is why Simni will not allow me in the temple, as I threaten the hierarchy and her way of doing things far too often. I lean into His teachings rather than her strict rules... and now I extend this offer to you. With how Rolandus is currently doing, now is the time to learn to help him." Letty stopped, found Marin's hand, and squeezed it. Neither spoke for several moments before Letty said, "He'll be okay. HaMelech is good and His power is mighty."

"Okay," Marin whispered.

Letty refreshed the water and then murmured, "Chittering sickness can make the injured manifest chitters. That's part of why Sinmi is so diligent in finding the biggest threat. It's dangerous to have many with chittering sickness, as it can compound and create an explosion of dread. As I said before, my friend will keep them at bay, but it is always something that can happen. I do not want you to be naïve to what we are dealing with here: if anything does happen, it can turn sour."

Marin nodded in diligent silence.

They returned to wiping the ichor from Rolandus' wounds before Marin wrapped them. Letty disappeared and then returned. "This is a lavender tincture... not quite the same as the one I gave him. Let's add this to the bandages to help heal and relax him. He felt tense as we cleaned his injuries, and he must relax before he can begin to rest. The issue with chittering sickness, and chittering madness, is that the venom causes severe distress. His muscles are tense, his mind is overactive, we need to address that to let him heal.... Rest will do you good as well, young lady. I have some other herbs we can add once you wake, but it can wait until then."

"I guess I can rest, but I should stay up with Rolandus to pray for him."

"Marin," Letty said, resting her hand on her arm, "if you don't rest, you will be unable to function tomorrow. Rest now, I will be here to pray over you both. I'll bring you something to eat, and I'll make sure that Rolandus is safe."

It took a few moments before Marin allowed Letty to escort her to the parlor. She laid down on the couch and Letty covered her with a blanket, "I'll wake you if anything happens, alright? Now, rest." She came back with a bowl of porridge for Marin and then left her alone.

After she ate, Marin lay awake for what felt like hours, her hands folded on her stomach as she stared at the ceiling. Eventually, she whispered, "HaMelech? I don't know what Your plan is, but I trust You. Your word is good, You are good, and You work all things for your good. Thank you so very much for bringing us to a place of safety and to someone who knows and loves You. I don't know what all happened with Grandma Letty and Madame Sinmi, but I know that it is in your will that I have met them both. Let me heed their words and let their hearts be moved according to your plan. Please, regardless of what happens, bring peace and healing to Rolandus so that he may return home with me. Bless Grandma Letty for her kindness, and heap blessings upon her more than she would ever expect... I love You, and I trust You."

A wash of peace settled over her and she nearly fell asleep before Rolandus whimpered in the other room. She laid still, listening, before she finally stood with the blanket around her shoulders and slipped back to the room Rolandus was in.

He was writhing slightly on the bed, under the covers. Letty was sitting beside him in a rocking chair, her eyes closed. Marin shifted, beginning to enter the room.

"Go back to sleep, Marin, I'm with him," Letty said. Marin paused at the woman's words.

She stared at her, and then Rolandus. "He isn't doing well. Please, may I stay with him?"

"I need you to rest," Letty said patiently. "If you don't take care of yourself, you won't be able to take care of him. Say goodnight and then go back to bed."

Marin sat on the edge of Rolandus' bed, gave him a gentle embrace to be certain that he was okay, and then slipped off. She fell asleep then, only waking as she smelled broth for breakfast.

Eating as fast as she could, Marin then hurried back to the bedroom. Letty had propped Rolandus up to give him broth. He didn't seem to know where he was, as he looked around between sips before his eyes landed on Marin. Recognition flooded his gaze as she sat on the bed edge beside him and then took his hand, but he didn't say anything. Marin reached out and cupped his cheek, searching his face. "Oh, Rolandus..."

"He's got open eyes, it's a good sign."

Marin glanced at Letty. "How do you know?"

"The slightest movement tells me what I need to know. Be a dear and open the blinds to let your wound sit in the sunlight. It'll likely hurt, but it'll make the venom fade. We'll need to do the same for Rolandus. Child, are you able to move to a chair or do you want to stay in bed?"

Rolandus didn't answer, his eyes closed. Marin squeezed his hand. "He's resting again."

"Then we will let him stay in the bed," Letty decided. "He needs to sleep as much as he can to fight the venom off. He feels less tense today, though, and that's a step."

For the next hour, Marin and Rolandus rested in a sunbeam. The black ichor on their wounds burned and thin wisps of smoke rose from the bile as it began to melt away in the light. Once the wounds had cleared, Marin climbed onto the bed beside Rolandus and curled up. He shifted near and she wrapped her arms around him, praying once more before she fell asleep.

She woke up before Rolandus did, drank some broth, and then wandered Letty's home to stretch her legs. The old woman sat in the parlor, running her finger over a book's page, and Marin crouched beside her. "What are you reading?"

"The Holy Texts." Letty didn't look up. "I don't often attend sermons anymore as it's hard for these old bones... but the pastor comes to my home and I've got several other women who visit to read the Word with me. My husband gave me this copy shortly after I lost my sight. If you look at it, you can see what I'm tracing and follow along with the written words."

"... may I read them with you, in Rolandus' room?" Marin asked. "I'm sure Rolandus would appreciate it if he heard, and I haven't had a chance to read the Holy Text in several days. I'm missing it."

Letty smiled. "That would be lovely, my dear."

They entered the room and Marin sat beside Rolandus, beginning to read from the texts. "And the Creator loved the world so much, that He gave His only begotten Son so that whoever believes in Him shall not perish, but have eternal life... Grandma Letty?"

"Hm?"

"What... happens to those who claim to believe in The Dove but do not act according to His will?"

Letty paused, tilting her head. "I suppose that is up to Him to decide when they enter His embrace, no? People will be turned away for what they believe, and that is between them and Him. Why?"

"I'm bitter about the temple and I hope they get what they have coming," Marin admitted. "Would HaMelech send them to hell for this?"

"Well," Letty paused for a moment, "it depends on what they did. When it comes down to it, people enter hell of their own choice. Yes, HaMelech passes the final judgment but it's the person's choices that ultimately determine where they go. And most importantly whether they have repented from their sins."

"I don't want to be angry at them for what they did, especially when I know they may yet repent," Marin sighed. She stared at the Holy Texts, skimming the words. "I suppose that part of me wants them to get what they deserve... and the other part of me hopes that they do repent."

"You're especially insightful."

Marin glanced at her, giving a bit of a smile. "My Da was a priest of HaMelech. He did deplorable things and broke my family, but he repented and was forgiven. I know that repentance is a part of being a Kingsman, but... it sometimes doesn't happen, and my heart breaks because of that."

Neither woman spoke and Marin took Rolandus' hand. His fingers twitched and she rubbed his hand. "I'm here, Rolandus."

"What happened in the temple, Marin?" Letty asked quietly. "Few run from the House of HaMelech unless something makes them... especially when you explained that HaMelech has been in your life since you were young."

"... They were going to remove Rolandus' injured limbs," Marin whispered. She stared at Rolandus. "And... and I didn't want that. I ran the moment that a chitter manifested, and that caused so many problems."

Letty frowned. "Marin, that is not enough to break the spirit in you. What happened?"

Marin shifted before she managed, "He was going to rape me."

The silence in the room was nearly deafening as Marin continued, "I ran because the knight keeping watch was going to rape me, and they were going to amputate and... and I didn't want any of that to happen. I know I caused my problems by running, and I didn't mean to release chitters in the temple but..." She stared at the bed, willing the covers to swallow her as she whispered, "I'm so, so sorry."

"Oh Marin." In an instant, Marin found herself in Letty's embrace. She tensed and then relaxed, starting to cry as Letty held her. "I'm so sorry, dear one. It isn't your fault that you ran: it was the safest option. You may have opened the door and let the chitters out, but that wasn't out of malintent. Look at me." Letty pulled away, cupping

Marin's chin. Even though Marin knew that the old woman couldn't see her, she knew that Letty was somehow searching her being. After a moment, Letty said, "You are a strong girl and one who wants the best for those around her. Nothing is your fault in this series of unfortunate events. You kept yourself safe, you were keeping Rolandus safe, and sometimes despite our best efforts others do receive happenings due to our actions."

"Maybe I should have let them take Rolandus and stayed out of it," Marin mumbled. "Then I wouldn't have released chitters."

"Young Master Rolandus does not need to have limbs removed. Look at him: tell me if you think taking away his ability to walk or use a weapon would fix the situation. Yes, we could have found ways to replace his limbs but would that have helped him? I'll give it to Sinmi and her Doves, as amputation is a safe, easy, and reliable way to take care of the issue but... Marin, I can hear his breathing is far better than when you first arrived. It is deeper and has settled. He will be alright. We can devote our full attention to his illness and injuries, something they cannot do."

Marin nodded, trying not to cry before Letty opened her arms again. She leaned into the woman, swallowing hard. After she had calmed down, Marin whispered, "Thank you. I'm sorry, I don't... everything feels like it's always my fault. My mother... when she was alive, she did her best to try soothing my worries and encourage me but then..." She trailed off. "My older brother does his best too, and so does Rolandus, but the voices keep telling me that I will never be enough and that it is always my fault."

"Those voices are not from HaMelech, but they are persuasive," Letty said. She brushed the hair from Marin's face. "When the time comes, He has instructed me to help open your eyes to what He sees. It may help you find your place in this broken world we live in. Until then, though, it's time to rest."

Marin nodded before she looked at Rolandus. He had calmed down and fallen asleep again, just as Letty had stated. The young redhead brushed her hand over his hair and he shifted towards her, making her sigh and place a feather-soft kiss on his forehead.

Letty stood up. "He will sleep easy tonight, and I assume he will do so tomorrow and the day after more than anything. We will feed him some broth in an hour and then, after he's well enough for us to leave his side, I will show you what you need to know when it comes to dealing with this illness."

CHAPTER THREE

Recovery

When Rolandus finally woke up, Marin was beside him, reading the Holy Texts aloud to both him and Grandma Letty. She looked at him when she felt a soft hand on her leg, her eyes growing wide and smile even wider as she realized that he was looking at her. "Rolandus... you're awake."

"How long have I been asleep?"

The woman put the book down, taking one of Rolandus' hands. "Do you remember me arriving in Last Hope?"

"Vaguely, but it's all hazy..."

"I arrived in Last Hope a week ago, a week and a day. We had to move you and the others from Last Hope and then we arrived here."

Rolandus' eyes flashed from Marin to Letty and he furrowed his brow. "Why aren't we in Apple Ridge?"

Marin explained to him what had happened with their travels, and what had happened before. As she did, Rolandus frowned deeper and deeper before he murmured, "So the rest of the caravan...?

"They left two days ago. I decided that we needed to stay to finish treating you."

"And... we aren't in the temple because...?"

The woman fell silent, beginning to fiddle with her skirt. Letty placed a gentle hand on Marin's shoulder. "I'm going to get you both something to eat."

Marin nodded remaining quiet until Letty left. Rolandus managed to sit up, though he groaned as his muscles protested. Marin could see tinges of black and red soaking into the bandages, but she was unable to chastise him as he stared at her.

"Marin, what happened?"

"... I took us from the temple," she whispered, "before you were able to be treated. They were going to amputate, and..." she stopped, staring at the floor. Tears began to fill her eyes and she finally mumbled, "There was a knight there, too, who... was less than kind."

Rolandus stared at her, his eyes narrowing. "How?"

Marin opened her mouth and then closed it. As hard as she tried, no words would come out. Instead, she began to cry. Rolandus' eyes widened and he opened his arms for her. Eventually, Marin managed, "You wouldn't really wake up, and I was afraid you wouldn't at all! And... and with everything that happened at the temple..." She began to sob again, managing to explain what had happened between arriving at the temple and then being found by Letty. As she did, Rolandus' grip tightened. She looked up at him, realized that there was a controlled rage in his eyes, and whispered, "I'm sorry..."

"I'm not upset with you," Rolandus said, his voice collected. "I am angry that someone would be so willing to abandon his promise to HaMelech in entering service, that he would be so tempted to harm a vulnerable young woman, and that I could do nothing about it." He was quiet for a moment. "Are you certain you're okay? He didn't hurt you?"

"... do you not believe me?"

"No! No, I do believe you but..." Rolandus trailed off. "I'm afraid that you're lying to keep focus off of yourself, as I know you care about me."

The woman shifted in his arms, shaking her head, and mumbled, "I wouldn't lie to you about this... I wouldn't lie to you ever."

"I will remember that," Rolandus whispered.

He held her close, rubbing her back before he laid back with Marin, holding her near. She kept her face in his chest, listening to his comforting heartbeat before she lifted her head, "I need to change your bandages."

"Don't change the topic. I need to ensure that someone knows about what happened," Rolandus said. He grit his teeth. "Vengeance may be HaMelech's, but I am also well aware of the need to repent or correct. Please, get me a parchment to write to the commanding knight here."

Marin shifted before she murmured, "I'm sorry, I didn't mean to cause such a big problem-"

"Marin, look at me."

She slowly met the man's eyes before he took her hand. Neither of them spoke for a moment before Rolandus said, "I want to do this for you because I care about you. I don't want anyone else to experience the same hurt and fear that you did, and I don't want there to be a potential of it happening again. As soon as I'm healed, we will leave. Until then, I want to do my role in being a knight of the Long Road and correct the mistakes others make around me just as they correct me."

They lay together for a few moments before Rolandus sighed and pressed his nose into Marin's hair. "You can take care of my bandages now if you would like."

"I need to." Marin sat up and began to undo his bandages, pulling the sticky cloth from each of the wounds. They were still oozing blood and ichor, though they looked better than they had before. They sizzled as the light touched them, making Rolandus wince, and Marin began to apply the various tinctures to a new set of bandages. As she reapplied them, Marin whispered, "I didn't know if I'd be returning to Apple Ridge with you..."

"Even if you buried me here, we would see each other again. It will be okay." Rolandus offered a little smile.

Marin paused, studying him, and then frowned. The black that had been covering his chest before, tangling towards his neck and around his heart, was still branching around. She touched one of the lines and he recoiled. As she stared at him, she mumbled, "I need Letty's advice... I don't know what to do. Does it hurt terribly?"

"Only when you touch it," Rolandus mumbled. He closed his eyes and Marin looked him over once more. The strange markings looked like they were pulsing, and the longer she stared at them the more she realized that the shadows were beginning to move. Gently, she took Rolandus' hand in her own.

He looked up at her. The amount of pain and fear in his eyes nearly brought Marin to tears. She swallowed past the lump in her throat. "It will be okay. HaMelech has you."

"I know." He offered a little smile again before he closed his eyes and shivered.

The young woman beside him tightened her grip on his hand, managed a breath, and whispered, "HaMelech, I don't know what to do and it scares me. Please, just... know that I trust you and I thank you for all that you've done. You are so much bigger than this, even if I feel like this is bigger than anything I've ever seen. You've brought us this far, You've kept us safe, and You've been beside us the entire time. You are a good Father, a good Friend, and a Comforter at a time when I know I need more than what this world offers. HaMelech, You are good and I trust you." Tears began to fall down Marin's face and she stared at Rolandus. He had fallen asleep again, prompting her to breathe, "Please, if it is in Your will, heal him. If... it isn't, then let me be by his side until the very end. I know that joining Your Embrace will bring him peace and a lack of pain but... it's so selfish of me to want him to stay if I'm merely asking for him to stay in a world of pain." She stared at the ceiling, trying to keep from sobbing, "I don't want to lose him, and I don't want to be disobedient to You. I want to keep him here with me, but I cannot fight the plan that you have in place. Help my heart prepare for what may come and keep my hands diligent so I may tend to Rolandus well while I hold him near."

Her throat tightened and she began to cry harder, unable to say anything else.

Letty wandered in with tea and broth after a few minutes. Rolandus drank with Marin's help, but there was no movement of his eyelids to show that he was awake. Marin held him close, staring at the wall as she rocked him.

"How do his wounds look?" Letty asked.

"They're getting worse. The black around his heart is moving and it hasn't gotten better even with the sunshine," Marin whispered. She swallowed. "I don't know if he'll make it through the night, given how bad this looks. He spoke to me, he seemed like he was doing okay, but he won't wake now. It's as though all the energy he did have is gone."

"I'm sorry sweetheart," Letty whispered. She was quiet for a moment before she murmured, "I'd like you to come into the attic with me, please."

"Why?"

"I feel like there is something there waiting for you and Master Rolandus that I need to get."

She made her way into the hallway and Marin followed. Once the ladder to the upper crawlspace was open, she followed Letty up. There, the young redhead looked around at various chests, folded linens, and items from an age gone by. Letty chuckled, "There's a lot up here, isn't there? Most of it is from my husband, HaMelech keep him, and still more is from my parents. This was the home I grew up in, and after my parents passed, I received it."

"Lots of memories," Marin murmured, looking around. "You said you're looking for one in specific?"

"Mhm..." Letty moved towards the back of the attic where she began to rummage, "Young Master Rolandus is an archer, isn't he?"

"He is. Olare should have the bow that Rolandus was using, it was his pride and joy. He spent hours on that bow," Marin said. "I just hope it wasn't broken; I've heard enough times that most people don't understand how much time goes into those weapons."

"Easy, Marin," Letty said. She lifted something and shook her head. "Things work in mysterious ways, and all things lost will be found in a new light." As she approached, she revealed a beautiful bow. Its maple wood glistened and, while it had no bowstring, it looked strong enough of a draw for Rolandus. Letty smiled, "This is a gift from HaMelech to my husband, and from me to your friend. I want you to give it to him, and I want him to know that it is a gift from HaMelech to you both."

"Both?"

Letty smiled. "Everything will be revealed in time, sweet girl. For now, all you need to know is that the bow is meant for you both. Now, I need you to return to him. It is time to lean into HaMelech with prayer and the Holy Texts."

Marin helped the woman from the attic and closed the hatch before she entered the room. Rolandus was lying on his back, his eyes closed, when she entered. It earned a smile from the girl as she entered and, after a moment, she began to place the bow against the wall.

As she did so, a quiet voice made her pause.

Put me with him.

The woman blinked, staring at the weapon, before yet another soft voice whispered, *"This is My will... rest My gift beside Rolandus."*

"HaMelech?" Marin breathed, standing still.

There was no other answer as she did as asked and placed the bow beside Rolandus. When she did, a soft golden sheen radiated off of the wood and seeped over his body. The chitter wounds began to fade and Rolandus sighed. Peace settled over his face and Marin felt an overwhelming sense of peace wash over her as well. Tears began to streak down her face and she fell to her knees, beginning to cry. "Thank you, HaMelech! Thank you for Your gifts, for Your healing, and Your Love! Thank you for hearing your servant's prayers and not turning from them. You work in such mysterious ways, and I can only praise you for what you are doing."

Rolandus didn't move as the bow glowed and Marin continued to cry, her sobs soon morphing into laughter of joy as she watched Rolandus' chest rise and fall more steadily than it had in a week.

This was a miracle.

Feeling better about Rolandus' state, Marin accepted Letty's invitation to work in the garden with her later that day. After several minutes, she asked, "Where did your husband receive the bow?"

"It appeared for him one day." Letty lifted her head and looked towards Marin. "It's a hardlight weapon, that much I know. He used it until the day he died."

"Aren't they usually buried with their user?"

Letty chuckled. "They are, and it was. I dreamt last night that it was in the attic and, when I awoke, I knew I needed to look. Sure enough, HaMelech returned it to this home for Rolandus to use."

Marin smiled and then paused, "Do they usually talk to people?"

"I wouldn't know, dear, but I know that they have a mind of their own... like chitter weapons."

"Grandma Letty... how do you know that?"

The old woman stopped, frowned, and then returned to looking for weeds. "When I was younger, I caught chittering madness. It started as the sickness, but as I was unable to receive help it only got worse. I manifested chitters, I knew no peace... and then one day I awoke without my sight. Whether it was an act of grace from HaMelech or an effect of the madness, I was able to function again without seeing chitters wherever I went. HaMelech has a beautiful plan for turning bad to good for those who love Him, and I now understand that this is why my sight was taken. I got married shortly thereafter and HaMelech began to use us to tend to those who have been infected. The Doves don't like me there, though, as I don't do things the way they do... I can't blame them, as HaMelech has shown me different methods than He has shown them, but it has become my calling. Now, I pass my knowledge onto you as He has asked me to. There is an herb that He blessed me with finding years ago, and I know that it is one that you must learn to grow and care for as you bring it from this place to the next as a part of your tools." They returned to tending to the plants, where Letty pointed out the strange yellow herb that Marin had first seen and used to wash Rolandus' injuries.

Letty was careful to show how to trim it back, placing the delicate flowers in Marin's hand with the promise of showing her how to use them.

After an hour, Marin returned to the bedroom where Rolandus lay.

Every so often, as the young woman ran a hand over his dreaded hair, he'd whine and then say her name. Marin sunk into the chair beside his bed again, took one of his hands, and pressed it to her forehead. "HaMelech... please be with him... You are mighty and are aiding him in recovery, and I thank you for all that you have done and all that you will do. Thank you for being a faithful God, thank you for being the great healer, and thank you for remaining close to us despite all that is happening."

She wasn't sure how long she had been sitting with Rolandus when Letty entered with two bowls of broth. As she rubbed a tender spot on her neck, she nodded at the old woman. "Thank you."

"Is he doing any better?"

Marin glanced at her friend. "He was, after I put the bow with him, but I'm worried he may be declining again."

"Hm," Letty murmured. She sat the second bowl of broth on the little bedside table and found Rolandus' hand. Then, ever so gently, she ran her touch up his arm until it rested on his forehead. His eyelids twitched though he didn't wake, and Letty closed her eyes. After a moment, she murmured, "He's still fighting, but HaMelech's strength surrounds him now in a different way. Would you like to see it?"

Letty held her hand out for Marin and the young healer took it. Letty said, "HaMelech, we thank you for the blessings You've given us and the healing that has taken place. Now, we ask you to open Marin's eyes to see the true battle taking place, as you have gifted me. Give her Your wisdom, that she may know what to do with this newfound knowledge, and help her to lean further into You as she learns the truth of the state of this world."

Marin glanced at Letty before a flash of movement in the corner of her eyes made her jump. Letty grabbed her arm. "Steady now, Marin. Take a breath and look at Master Rolandus."

A man was sitting on the bed beside Rolandus, a golden sheen radiating from him. His white hair was slicked back as he focused on Rolandus, specifically his head. He didn't spare Marin or Letty a glance, though he smiled as though he realized that Marin could see him. His hands rested on Rolandus' brow, emanating the sheen, and he closed his eyes after a moment.

Marin stared at the newcomer, and then at Letty before movement in the corner of her eye made her whip around again.

Against the wall was a swirling form of shadows. It crept towards them, stalking on all fours, and Marin nearly screamed if not for Letty's quiet voice, "It has no power here, child. This is a home dedicated to the King of Kings. This is why your friend is battling. Forces of HaMelech surround us every day, guiding our hands and acting in His will, while the Black Dragon attempts to slither into our hearts and minds to claim us as his victims. Chittering sickness, chittering madness, is more than an illness. It is a battleground, where creatures cling to the ill and do their best to consume and rob every aspect that HaMelech has made good... all the while, HaMelech's army is fighting on our behalf.

"This is why the Solari are unable to help those who are suffering from this and instead kill. They don't have the gift to see into the spirit realm... and they don't call upon the power of our God. Instead, they allow the Black Dragon to whisper lies into their ears where they succumb to it."

"There are so many things... hidden things... that surround us, Grandma Letty," Marin whispered. She glanced at the older woman, aware of tears streaking down her face. "Don't they frighten you?"

"They did, once," Letty said, "but then I learned to look for my friends through the darkness. You are one, young Master Rolandus is another... as is our visitor protecting us. The more you focus on the shadows, the more power you are giving them. They feed off of your fear and anxiety, Marin, where we know there is no fear in following HaMelech. He is holding you in His righteous right hand, and He will not let you fall. It is focusing on His word, His goodness, and His might that allows us to travel through this warfare... and I want you to experience this before you leave. Look at me, Marin."

As the young woman looked at Letty, Marin found that the other had developed a look of contentment and peace. Though Letty couldn't see her, the faintest glimmer of recognition flooded Letty's eyes now that they were looking at each other with this gift. Marin shifted and Letty took her hand. "HaMelech has blessed you with such a beautiful, receptive spirit. This gift is to bring you closer to Him, alright?"

Marin nodded, looked around the room again, and then whispered, "Why hadn't HaMelech allowed me to see this before?"

"He is a good Father, and that means protecting His children from frightening things until they're ready to face them. In your case, this is something that you can use to help people like young Master Roland us... people who need intersession to receive healing as they're unable to pray for themselves. You trust Him so deeply, and I hear your prayers each time I pass this room. This is the next step in becoming what He has called you to be, dear child." Letty kissed the top of Marin's head, smiling. "Your friend will be recovering for a few weeks yet, and after he does, you will be returning home. Until then, it is my task to ensure that you are prepared for when you step into your calling."

Marin nodded and the two fell silent, watching the shadows that attempted to creep through the windows or under the door towards Rolandus.

The man slept as the stranger above him remained, and Marin watched as the stranger continued to pass his hands over Rolandus' temples. She finally dared, "Have you been here this entire time?"

There was no answer, but the stranger smiled as though her question amused him. He didn't look up, either, but Marin could tell that he was watching her out of the corner of his eye. Without anything else to do, and the knowledge that prayer was one of the few things that she could do, Marin took her friend's hands and began to pray over him again.

It was then that the stranger looked at her, the smile never leaving his face. Marin met his eyes, offered a little smile back, and then returned to her prayer.

Eventually, she noticed the stranger vanish- more precisely, transform into a small glowing orb and then disappear- as the shadows creeping towards her grew darker. She held tighter to Rolandus' hand before she took a breath. "HaMelech is bigger than the darkness around us... His hand steadies my walk, His footsteps are beside mine. I am His daughter, His prize, His bride... the darkness has no power over me as I know whose I am."

The shadows seemed to recoil and Marin, as they redoubled their efforts, found her tongue locking in place.

Panic began to rise in her chest before unknown words tumbled past her lips. In a whirlwind, peace settled over her, tears began to streak down her cheeks as she let out a sob, and the darkness, as though a match had been lit under it, fled.

Gifts are given if you ask, child... and for you and my children, I wish to give you the most beautiful I have... take this tongue, speak to My Breath.

Marin began to cry harder. "HaMelech..."

I am well pleased, good and faithful servant, and I am with you. Always.

The voice faded away as Marin cried, holding onto Rolandus' hand and whispering in the unknown tongue she had been gifted with. Rolandus tightened his grip and shifted, slowly opening his eyes to stare at Marin. She met his gaze. "Rolandus..."

"Hey... you've been crying," he whispered. He studied her and then reached out to cup her cheek. "Why are you crying?"

"You're okay... I can't believe you're awake!" Marin said. She rested her hand on his own, holding tightly to the one she was still holding, and swallowed. "I was afraid you weren't going to wake up again and after everything..."

"Sh, it's alright. I'm okay, Marin, I'm alright." Rolandus tried to sit up before he gasped and lay down again.

She rested her hand on his chest. "Stay still, let me tend to you; you're still injured and need to rest."

He clung to her, shaking, before he caught sight of the bow on the bed. "Where did that come from?"

"It's a gift from Letty. It's a hardlight bow."

Rolandus hummed in interest. "Please, can you get it for me?"

As soon as he had it in his hand, the man inspected it. "It's beautiful."

"It was her husband's, and it showed back up after he passed. She wanted us... you... to have it."

Marin shifted as he looked at her, a little smile playing on his lips, and then watched as he lifted it with redouble strength and mimed drawing a bowstring back. All at once, a beautiful bowstring and blazing arrow appeared. Marin's eyes widened at the sight before Rolandus relaxed his arm and allowed the golden string back to its original place, where it vanished once more. Then, they shared a glance and began to laugh at the blessing they were given without any asking or notice.

"Praise HaMelech!"

Rolandus laid down and slept for several hours after Marin changed his bandages, the bow beside him, and Marin read the Holy Texts out loud. Her mind wandered for the majority of it, though she did her best to keep focused. Eventually, Marin closed the book and rested a hand on Rolandus' forehead.

She closed her eyes and began to pray, "HaMelech, thank you for your mercy and your grace. Thank you for healing Rolandus, thank you for protecting us in the streets." Rolandus shifted under her touch and she opened her eyes to see that he was looking at her. Quietly, she held his hand and smiled at him before she closed her eyes again. "You are so much bigger and stronger than the troubles of this world, and we are blessed to be Your children. Thank you for faithfulness, thank you for friendship..."

"Thank you for sending me help," Rolandus whispered.

They remained with Letty for four more days.

Rolandus spent most of the time resting and regaining his strength, though he took the last day to sit outside in the sun while Marin gardened. Every so often, he'd glance at Marin and she'd meet his eyes, smiling before she'd turn back to her work. As it approached noon, she sat back on her heels. Letty had gone inside to prepare lunch, leaving the two alone beneath the sun. Rolandus shifted in his chair, wincing as his muscles protested. "Why don't you come sit, Marin?"

"I suppose I can for a few minutes." Marin stood, brushing her hands onto the apron Letty had lent her. "It's time to eat, anyway." She crossed to her friend and sat beside him, sighing as the sunshine dappled over her face. "How are you feeling?"

Rolandus was quiet for a moment. "Tired, conflicted, ready to return home. How about you?"

She glanced at him, one brow raised. "Ready to be back... what are you conflicted about?"

Once more, Rolandus didn't speak. Finally, he murmured, "I'm conflicted about how I feel when I'm around you, and the actions I'm taking about those feelings." He shifted, meeting her eyes, "The last couple of days... weeks, even... have shown me how much I care about you and how frightened I am of losing you. I also know that I don't want to take these feelings for granted, nor do I want to lean so heavily into them if they're merely coming from what's happened to us." Marin's face grew hot and she tucked a strand of hair behind her ear. Rolandus sighed, "I don't want to hurt our friendship."

"Of all the times to bring something like this up, you've chosen shortly after you nearly died, when we're miles away from home, wondering if my brother is alright?" Marin asked.

Rolandus choked before he rubbed the back of his neck. "I suppose it's not the best time, is it?"

Marin giggled and shook her head. "It could have been worse." She sighed, looking over the garden and the cottage they had been staying in. Homesickness surrounded her, along with a twinge of guilt, before she looked back at her friend. He was watching her quietly, his dark eyes gentle, and a smile on his lips. He had left his mantle inside, but Marin knew that the curiosity he had in his gaze would remain regardless of the form he took. Peace settled over her. "I do love you." His eyes grew wide and she continued, "I love you dearly, more than I could ever explain. HaMelech brought you into my life for a purpose, and I am grateful each day that He did. As much as I want to say that we should be together, that we should build a family together, I don't want to step into a life that isn't blessed by HaMelech or Olare. I love them very much too, and I want to be certain that we are being obedient to our King and that my brother agrees with our union."

They stared at each other and then Rolandus took Marin's hands. He smiled at her, and she returned it before he sighed and rested his forehead against her own. "Then I want us to both pray about it and seek out HaMelech's guidance... each of us in our private devotions. I want nothing more than this to be a 'yes', but I know that the last thing I want to do is turn you towards what I want."

Marin squeezed his hands. "Alright, then it's settled." She pulled away from him, smiling, and then shifted. "Thank you for being such a dear friend at the very least. Even if the answer is 'no', I don't want to lose our friendship."

Rolandus smiled as Letty called from inside. They ate a light lunch with her, speaking quietly, before she presented Marin with a pouch of herbs and a little journal. "This is for you, Marin. I've packed some of the Valri seeds for you to bring home with you to create a garden. You know how to tend to them now, and you're always welcome to return to me should you need more. The journal has some more notes and techniques for you as well. I've included my address if you want to write."

"Thank you," Marin said. She stared at the tiny seeds, inhaling the light smell of cinnamon, and then looked at the elder. "Are you sure?"

"Of course I am. It's time for you to return home and bring this with you." She looked at Rolandus. "Use the bow well: it is a great friend in times of trouble. Rest today and tomorrow. I will gather rations for you to take with you."

CHAPTER FOUR

New Orders

For most of the trip to Apple Ridge, Marin slept. The other part was spent in quiet meditation or reading the Holy Texts with Rolandus. Neither of them spoke about their conversation regarding a relationship. Marin kept silent in an attempt to focus on HaMelech and Rolandus... well, she assumed it was for the same reason.

The wagon jolted as they stopped. The apple orchards around them were a welcome sight. Marin glanced at Rolandus. "We're home... I've never been gladder to be home before."

"I know... what a way to have my first patrol in Bleak Hollow go," Rolandus said. They glanced at each other, shared an uneasy laugh, and then got out of the wagon together.

Several people came to greet them, one of whom was Sister Iren, and Marin embraced each. After the 'hellos', she looked around. "Is Olare still serving?"

"He should be returning home any day," Iren replied.

Rolandus rested a hand on Marin's back. "Let's get you home, then, so you can rest before he arrives. I'm sure he's going to keep you up until the wee hours talking about what happened once we left Last Hope."

Marin glanced at him. "I'd like to, but I should go with Sister Iren to discuss chittering sickness. From what I can tell, we don't have any of the setup we need to treat people with it... and I know that you'll still need treatment until further notice."

Her friend stared at her before his eyes softened and he nodded. "Alright. Is there anything I can do to help you?"

The woman shook her head. "I appreciate you asking, and I would happily accept your help if I had anything you could do."

"May I come with you and watch, then?"

Iren followed them as they made their way to the temple and Marin began to explain what she had learned from Letty. Iren listened intensely. "We'll begin to modify the wing that most of our chittering madness... sickness... patients go to."

Rolandus remained by Marin's side, finally resting a hand on her back. Marin glanced at him, smiled, and then turned back to Iren.

After several hours, the two went back to Marin's home where she began dinner. They sat quietly, listening to the fire pop.

Rolandus hummed, tapping his leg. It took him a few minutes before he said, "I'm glad you ended up in Last Hope when you did. I'm even more glad to know that Letty has been teaching you what to do. Have you been enjoying what you've learned?"

The redhead glanced at him, watching as he looked around the room and then his gaze focused on her. They held each other's stare for a moment, breaking it only when Marin said, "I need to take tonight to continue to pray."

"Then take tonight and tomorrow, too," Rolandus replied. He shifted. "I don't want to step into something that'll only hurt us."

Marin smiled at him, paused, then took his hand in her own. They sat in silence as they watched the fire burn. Rolandus lightly rubbed her hand with his thumb before he murmured, "The sheepdogs should start whelping, soon."

"Are you planning on doing most of the training?"

"I think so," Rolandus said. He sighed. "It's silly, but did you know it's one of the ways I try to honor my parents' memories? They've been gone for 10 years but..." Marin squeezed his hand and he offered a small smile. "I guess I just want to be as much like them as I can. They would have loved you, you know? Mother especially; I know she spent each night praying for me and those I'd meet along the way. I don't think she ever foresaw what happened, but I know that they're in good hands now."

He fell silent and Marin shifted closer, resting her head on his shoulder to offer what comfort he could. It was then that she realized he had begun to cry, prompting her to turn and embrace him. He leaned into her and she simply held him, stroking his hair as she murmured to him, "HaMelech is holding them. I know they are waiting for you... for us... once we join HaMelech as well." He nodded slightly and she tightened her grip, taking deep breaths as she did so. Eventually, she began to whisper in the newfound tongue she received while with Letty. Rolandus shifted as she did so, but he didn't comment on it. Instead, his sniffles died down and he remained in her arms as he listened to her quiet words.

Finally, Rolandus pulled away from her. He stared at her for a moment, fondness in his eyes, and then murmured, "You have a beautiful spirit, Marin." For a moment, he didn't move. Then, he abruptly stood and crossed the room. "I should probably leave you to your evening. Olare's due to be home any day now, and we want to take some additional time to pray."

Marin furrowed her brows and nodded. She followed him to the door. "Are you certain you don't want to stay to eat?"

Rolandus paused, halfway outside. He shifted once, sighed, and looked at her. "I want to, but I'm worried that I'm going to make poor choices if I do. I..." He trailed off, his cheeks becoming red. "I want you,

Marin, and I'm afraid that if I stay with you any longer tonight then I will take advantage of you and our friendship and... I'm afraid that if I do attempt to do so, you wouldn't necessarily stop me."

Marin's face grew hot at his words and she looked away. "Thank you for being honest. I think it's a wise decision." She cleared her throat. "At very least, are you willing to let me send you home with dinner? It's done, and I don't want it to go to waste."

He nodded and she hurried to dish a steaming bowl of stew for him. He took it, offered her a soft smile and 'goodnight' before he slipped away.

After she had locked the door and eaten, Marin knelt before her bed in silence.

She didn't say anything for the longest time, finally breathing, "HaMelech" after what felt like an eternity. Though there was nothing around her, the stillness seemed to welcome her with open arms. The shadows were quiet, unmoving, and Marin took a deep breath into the calm.

She wasn't alone. All around her, she could feel the gentle presence of HaMelech. It was a feeling she had to learn over time, especially when she was younger. She knew He was always there, but calming her body and mind to feel His presence required practice. It was a sense of peace in the raging storm of life, a knowledge that it would be okay regardless of what happened.

Marin took a breath again, this time murmuring, "I want to seek Your will. You have gifted me with a friendship that I love, and a man who I love more deeply than I can describe. Your gifts are perfect, and You have given me so much more than I could ever express gratitude for." She paused, letting the stillness wash over her again, and then whispered, "You are a good Father, and a faithful Friend. Your mercy and grace are gifts that I cannot begin to fathom, and I am so grateful for what You sent Your son, the Dove, to do. Your will is perfect... and I want to follow it, even if it means turning away from my wants. But... HaMelech, is it in Your will to move forward with Rolandus? To enter a life with him as his wife and... build a family? Or is it against all that You're calling me to do?"

As she sat there, tears began to fall down her face. She didn't move, though, and continued to sit in silence as she waited for something to answer her. Finally, the faintest feeling of a new calm washed over her.

Marin began to cry harder, taking in shaking breaths as the sudden and overwhelming realization of it being okay struck her.

Now what did she do? What was it going to look like?

She returned to prayer before a heavy knock sounded on the door. Marin grabbed her hunting knife from her nightstand and crept to the entry. "Who is it?"

"Marin, it's Olare. I'd like in, please."

Marin paused and then scrambled with the lock. "You're home!"

She flung herself into his arms and held onto him. Olare stumbled slightly. "Of course I'm home! It was time to return. I didn't think you'd be so happy to see me... were you crying? What happened, what's wrong?"

Marin shook her head, instead clinging to her brother until she finally pulled away. "It doesn't matter. You're home, things are moving according to HaMelech's will, and it's alright. Do you need something to eat? I have some stew in the pot from dinner. I'm happy to heat it up before you rest."

"No, that's alright. Are you sure everything's okay?"

"Perfectly!" Marin smiled at him, taking his hands to pull him inside before she shut the door. "I can cry happy tears, Olare, and these were happy tears. I'm just... HaMelech is so wonderful and gracious, and I can hardly believe it. He's spoken beautiful news to me before you returned."

Her brother paused as he took off his boots. "Are you able to share the news, or is it for you alone?"

"I would, but I need to wait until I hear from Rolandus first."

The words made Olare smile slightly. He returned to his boots, placed them by the door, and then pulled off his heavy cloak. "Would it happen to be something involving our dear friend?"

"Perhaps, but that is all you will receive from me." Marin took his cloak. "Was the trip here okay? We had no trouble coming from Godrick's Rest today, but-"

"Godrick's Rest?" He stopped again, this time as he crossed to the wash basin. "Only today? You left Last Hope nearly a week ago: why did you take so long to return here?"

Marin looked at him. "We had to stay due to Rolandus' chittering sickness." Olare's gaze didn't leave her as she went to the fire and poked at the coals, breathing on them to light them, "It was getting worse when we had left Last Hope, and if we hadn't stopped at Godrick's Rest then I fear he would be suffering even now."

"Is he alright then?"

"Mostly. He's still got some recovery to go, but it is a matter of calming his nerves and allowing HaMelech's power to work over him." Marin looked at her brother. "We spent most of the time with a woman named Leticia... Grandma Letty. She spent years learning how best to tend to those with chittering madness or chittering sickness. I'm planning on planting some of the herbs she sent me with tomorrow so we can begin changing our practices... what do I need to slow down on?"

"Everything. You had someone show you what to do for chittering madness? Why weren't you at the temple?"

Marin sat back on her heels, looked at the ceiling, and then said, "We left the temple when the only treatment option was amputation."

"Amputation?"

"Yes." She looked back at the coals, trying to get them to light, and then stopped. After several moments of silence, Olare watching her the entire time, she finally sighed. "There... was also a knight there who..." she trailed off, shifted, and shook her head, "Rolandus took care of it, but we left because of that, too. It wasn't great; there were chitters, and I was bitten, and..." she trailed off again, suddenly aware of tears pricking her eyes. "Olare, I caused a lot of problems while I was there."

Her brother frowned, shook his head, and started to wash his hands. "No, your response to others caused problems. Whatever happened, I know you did nothing out of spite or malice- you aren't that type of person, and I can only imagine that you took the best actions based on what was happening."

He wiped his hands and then sat by Marin. "Honestly, I figured that Rolandus was going to lose a limb. There aren't many options for chittering madness, and that was something I knew in sending him to Godrick's Rest. They had a better chance at keeping him alive, though."

"Well... I didn't like it. He's home, he left several hours ago to rest, but he is home and still able to serve." Marin sighed and poked at the fire. "I just... feel guilty still."

"HaMelech knows your heart, Marin, and He knows the reason behind what happened."

They retired for the night, where Marin spent a few more minutes in prayer before she fell asleep.

Olare joined her at the temple the next morning. When they moved to the new ward for chittering sickness, he gave a hum of approval. "You're heading this up, then? Are you having anyone help you?"

The woman shifted and then shook her head. "Not yet, but I'll be training people to help, or at least know what to do. Rolandus has been doing what he can to help, he did so yesterday."

"Do you know where he is now?"

Marin shook her head, received a kiss on her head from her brother, and then watched him hurry off. He paused halfway through the door, turned, and said, "I'll be back in a bit. I need to talk to him, especially about what happened while he was gone."

She returned to what she was doing as Olare hurried out again. After an hour, Olare came back, this time with Rolandus. Marin smiled as she saw them, her smile growing wide as Rolandus took her hand and sat beside her. Olare cleared his throat and then sat beside them as well. "So... Rolandus filled me in on Godrick's Rest."

Marin rubbed her thumb over Rolandus' hand. "We were alright once Grandma Letty took us in, but it was still touch and go. I'm grateful that HaMelech placed us with someone who has been working so diligently on treating chittering sickness."

"Hm," Olare hummed. He gave a bit of a nod before he said, "Well, Marin, as our resident expert.... has Rolandus made a full recovery?"

The woman looked back at Rolandus, studying his face. He had filled out again, no longer as gaunt as he had been when she first saw him in Last Hope. As she watched, she caught his eyes dart to a single corner of the room, his grip tightening ever so slightly on her hand.

She squeezed his hand, and then murmured, "Mostly. It's the fading memories left; more sunlight and comfort will help chase the phantoms away. He's able to return to patrol and serving now, it shouldn't cause any issues there."

"It isn't bad," Rolandus said. "It's just... flits of movement in the corner of my eye. It's startling, but that's all it is."

Olare nodded in approval and then stood. "Then I expect to see you tomorrow morning, Rolandus, on the field. I still need to give my report: I'll see you both for supper."

He started to the door before he looked at them again. "Rolandus also spoke to me about something he'd like to ask you. I want to give you this warning: if you do anything to harm her, Rolandus, I will deliver you to HaMelech for judgment."

"I would never harm Marin, Olare, you know this." Rolandus smiled at the man and Olare returned the gesture. He then looked down at Marin. "HaMelech has shown me that this is the path I am to take, and Olare gave his blessing. So... I don't have a ring, or much to my name, but I have a warm home and a love that surpasses anything I've experienced in this world. HaMelech knows my heart, He knows my desire to be with you, and He has been kind to allow me to ask you to be my bride. Marin, will you marry me?"

Marin rested her forehead against Rolandus'. "Nothing would make me happier, Rolandus. I love you with all my being."

Quietly, the two sat before Rolandus murmured, "HaMelech, thank you for blessing this union and this friendship. Your gifts are astounding and so much better than we could ever assume. Thank you for Marin and her gentle spirit, and thank you for the wisdom that she brings me. I am so incredibly blessed to be able to call her fiancé and soon to be wife, even more so knowing that I can love her to the best of my capabilities." He squeezed Marin's hand. "We ask that You continue to bless our life together and demonstrate Your power in our lives, and remind us that You are first in our marriage."

Marin nodded as Rolandus prayed, though she didn't say anything as he did.

They remained together for a little bit before Rolandus had to go, leaving Marin to finish setting up. Eventually, she made her way to the sanctuary once she was content with her work.

For a moment, all she did was sit in silence.

It was nice to be able to do this, especially after so long. Eventually, Marin whispered, "I missed this. I missed being able to sit in Your presence, and being able to focus on You rather than a thousand other things alongside You. Thank you for keeping us safe throughout our travels and thank you for bringing Olare home. So many things could have gone wrong. Rolandus might not have made it, or Olare could have died... so thank you for getting my family home safe."

Marin remained before the altar for an hour, whispering prayers under her breath. After a little bit, she stood and left.

It was supper time when she found Rolandus waiting to escort her home. They sat as Olare finished making the meal, where he looked at them. "So, are you engaged?"

"If we weren't, you would have ruined the surprise," Rolandus said with a grin.

Olare chuckled, "It wouldn't have been a surprise; we all knew that it was only a matter of time." He held out a bowl to each of them. "Congratulations, regardless. I know HaMelech has plans for you both, and I'm excited to see what comes of it."

Marin smiled at Rolandus as Olare continued, "Rolandus, have you had a chance to check in on the sheepdogs since you got back?"

"No. I was under the impression that you wanted me to do other duties now."

"Not at all," Olare answered. He sat, took a bite of his food, and waved his spoon slightly. "I want you to continue working with them... more so now than ever. Rolandus, you have a unique gift in being able to train them. They trust you, and the fact that you can give whistle commands as needed shows me that you would do excellent in continuing this. Of course, I still need you to attend training and to assist me with our archers, but the sheepdogs are your projects."

Rolandus' face lit up as he beamed. "Thank you, Olare! Marin, would you be able to help me with the sheepdogs when you're able? I know that you're a Dove, but having your gentle temper would help too."

The woman nodded. "Of course, Rolandus. I know how special the sheepdogs are to you."

That night, after Rolandus had finished eating with them, he bid Marin and Olare a goodnight and left. Marin sighed, beginning to brush her hair out. "Olare?"

"Yes?"

"What are you going to do once Rolandus and I are wed?"

Her older brother looked up from his whittling project and said, "Relegate myself to being Uncle Olare one of these days. Nothing is going to change outside of Rolandus taking care of you now, and even then he always has." The man sat for a moment. "I owe him for that, though that isn't why I agreed with him asking you. He's taken care of you since the two of you met and I'm so grateful that he did when... well, we both know that I could have done better. I see how much he loves you, and I know that he'll be good to you."

"Are you going to miss everything we had before?"

"Miss you tormenting me? No, Marin. It's a new season of life, and I'm happy for you. HaMelech has something in store for you, Rolandus, and myself that I will never understand. Right now, though, it's wise to begin to rest for the night. We've had long travels, each of us, and the sooner we can recover, the sooner we are useful."

Marin smiled at him as he ruffled her hair. "I love you, Marin. I'm glad that Rolandus will be taking his place by your side."

"Thank you for everything, Olare. I love you too."

Marin was ready for bed when a frantic knocking sounded on the door. She grabbed her hunting knife from her bedside table and hurried to the door as Olare stumbled from his bed. "Who is it?"

"I don't know."

She opened the door to see Rolandus. He was breathing hard, one hand on his knee as he doubled over himself.

"Rolandus?"

"Marin... Marin, I'm sorry, but I need your help. I went to... to check on the sheepdogs and..."

"Okay, hang on..." Marin pulled on her dressing robe, shawl, and boots, "Is everything okay?"

"No... no, it isn't... one of the dogs...."

There was no explanation before Marin took off after Rolandus. Olare called after her that he could get someone else to help but she was already gone before she could shout back.

Rolandus heaved open the heavy doors of the barn where they kept the sheepdogs and Marin hurried in. "What... Oh, no..."

One of the sheepdogs had gone into labor. She had three puppies beside her but hadn't begun to lick them. Rolandus began to rub the puppies. "I don't know what you can do but... but I need your help. No one was here, they should have been keeping an eye on them!"

"It's going to be okay, Rolandus..." Marin approached the sheepdog, doing what she could. After several minutes, she finally whispered, "She's too far gone."

Her fiancé looked at her, tears beginning to streak down his face. "Then what do we do with her puppies?"

Two of them were moving, and the third was still. Marin pulled her shawl off and began to wipe the living pups down. "Is there another sheepdog with pups?"

"Not this young," Rolandus said. "They're all several weeks older, so the milk won't be right for this stage."

"Well... have you reared puppies before?"

"It's been years."

"Get a bottle then, I'll keep these two warm," Marin whispered.

The sheepdog stopped breathing as Rolandus turned away, and Marin ran a hand over its fur with a sigh. This was a hard night.

The young man returned to her side and noticed the still dog. He didn't say a word and instead moved closer to Marin, trying to coax either pup into accepting the bottle. She rested her head on his shoulder, watching as one of the puppies finally took the bottle and began to nurse. The other puppy struggled for a few moments before it, too, began to drink from the bottle. Rolandus sighed, "They'll be okay if they can make it through the first night. I'm sorry I pulled you from your home-"

"Rolandus, my love, this is something that you needed help with. I would rather help you with this than you to have no aid." Marin looked at him and then settled her head on his shoulder again. "I'm so sorry we were too late."

"This happens, but... I know it could have been avoided," Rolandus mumbled. "If I had been here sooner-"

"No, Rolandus. This isn't on you. You were not scheduled to be with the sheepdogs today."

"I could have checked, though."

"This isn't your fault."

He sighed and nodded, though Marin could that that he didn't believe her. She paused and then gave his temple a gentle kiss. "Rolandus, you do a good job taking care of the sheepdogs. This was an accident."

"A dog... two dogs... still died."

"You will put precautions in place to avoid this from happening again," Marin murmured.

They remained together before Rolandus shifted. "When do you want to get married?"

"I haven't thought that far ahead," Marin said, offering a little chuckle. "Why?"

Rolandus shifted. "Well..." He sighed after a moment. "I feel ridiculous, but I know there are lines that we can't cross... but I..." His face grew crimson as he mumbled, "There are some temptations that I'm currently dealing with, and I don't want to succumb to them."

Marin sat up. "I don't want to drive you to stumble, either... but I don't think getting married soon is a good idea. I want to plan things; we're going to have to be sure we have a home to ourselves. I know you've got roommates, and I live with my brother, and we can't oust either of them. We need a home, and in getting a home we will need to plan for a family-"

"A family, hm?" Rolandus interrupted. Marin flushed and Rolandus chuckled. "I want to have a family with you, I just wasn't thinking that far ahead." They looked down at the puppies before Rolandus whispered, "I am willing to wait as long as we need to, and longer if that is what HaMelech calls us to do. My heart is for you, and no others."

Marin shifted. "My heart, my soul, and my body are yours. I do not want to make a promise too lightly as we wait for our wedding. Until then... I vow to be yours, and yours alone. HaMelech is my groom until we can join hands in marriage, and then we will serve together. I will not think of any other, nor will I bond with another aside from you."

Rolandus stared at her before he responded, "Are you certain, Marin? If something happens... you are vowing celibacy until we-"

"I know, and that is what I want. I will be yours, faithfully, regardless of what happens," Marin said.

Her fiancé nodded, leaned in, and pressed his forehead to her own. Marin closed her eyes to savor the feeling as he whispered, "Then I pledge my heart, soul, and body to you. Until we wed, HaMelech is my portion and I am yours just as you are mine. I swear to serve our King by your side, even if our time to wed has yet to pass. I love you, Marin, and I will continue to love you until the day I die."

They fed the puppies until Marin yawned and leaned against Rolandus again. He wrapped an arm around her to keep her near, continuing to dote on the tiny creatures he held in his hand.

"I should get you home, Marin," Rolandus said, startling Marin. She looked at him and he chuckled, "Come on, it's time for you to rest. There is much for you to do tomorrow, I'm sure, and I have my hands full with these pups until further notice."

"Rolandus?"

"Yes?"

Marin looked at the sky as they left the barn. "Do... you think this is the right thing to do?"

"What?"

"Celibacy... until HaMelech's timing is right?"

Rolandus shifted before he nodded. "I am yours until that day if you are still willing to be mine. Should something happen, and we are released from this promise, then it will no longer be the right thing to do."

Marin stepped to her door and then studied Rolandus. His brown eyes were tired and he offered an exhausted smile. The puppies, now tucked in his tunic and wrapped in her shawl, wriggled and whimpered, "I love you. Good night, Rolandus."

"Good night, Marin. Sleep well."

She watched as he disappeared into the darkness, feeling a sudden weight on her chest.

Something was coming, something that frightened her. Marin felt the hunting knife at her hip, and then stepped into her darkened home.

Olare was snoring in his bed and Marin, after several minutes, settled into her bed. She stared at the rafters, listening to her brother breathe heavily, and then whispered, "HaMelech... I don't know what your plan is, but if something must happen... please, let it be known. I'm here, waiting, and I am obedient to your word. Just tell me what to do, and I will move."

The silence around her was deafening until a still, quiet voice spoke. It was as though it was the wind itself, hushed and soothing, as it carried a single word.

"Zanther."

Marin furrowed her brow before she whispered, "Zanther?"

Nothing answered and Marin, fully awake again, drew her dressing gown over her nightgown, and then left her home again.

It was silent as she hurried through the streets, her eyes adjusting to see the white stone of HaMelech's temple ahead of her. She slipped inside, shut the heavy oak door behind her, and then made her way to the altar.

There were no others within the sanctuary. Marin sank before the altar, stared at the wall, and then sat.

Despite the silence, Marin knew that something was speaking to her. She peered through the darkness, finding that there were a handful of shadows that had begun to creep towards her as they did in Godrick's Rest. Then, she shut her eyes. "HaMelech, I need your guidance.

"I don't know why I've heard Your voice, but I want to be obedient to your call. If I am to go to Zanther, I need a sign: give me something that I cannot deny as You, so I may know that this is Your will."

She remained quiet for a few more moments before she whispered, "I trust you, and I love you. You are holy, You are sovereign, You are good."

Once she was finished with her prayer, she returned home only to wake up several hours later.

Olare's voice filled the cottage as he spoke, "I'm not about to suggest that my sister go alone, Rolandus-"

"Olare, I know, and I don't want her to either but... I can't deny the dream I had. I don't know if it'd be better for you to mention it or if I should: I don't want to break her heart, not... not when we're planning on getting married."

"This had better not be cold feet!"

Marin pulled on her dressing robe and hurried from her bed, opening the door from the bedchambers to see the two men.

Rolandus had the two puppies in his lap, wrapped with a blanket as he bottle-fed them. Olare, meanwhile, paced the room. As Marin entered, they stopped and looked at her. "Marin!"

"You were loud, Olare. What's going on, what dream are you talking about?" The men stopped what they were doing and looked at her.

Marin glanced between them, pulled her robe a little closer to herself, and frowned. "One of you needs to speak up-"

"Go on, Rolandus, it's your dream."

Marin looked at her fiancé as he sighed, lowering his gaze to the ground. "We need to postpone everything. I had a dream last night that you need to go... alone... to one of the major cities. I don't know which one it was, and I tried to go with you, but my path was blocked. You looked back at me, told me that it was okay, and I watched you leave." Rolandus shifted. "Olare and I think it's from HaMelech, but unless there's confirmation-"

"This was confirmation, Rolandus," Marin said. She began to stoke the fire. "HaMelech said 'Zanther' last night and I asked for confirmation. I don't know why I need to go there, I haven't had any next steps given, but I had a feeling that I would hear something today about this."

Olare held his hand up. "So you were planning on going to Zanther alone?"

"If HaMelech confirmed that I heard His voice, yes," Marin replied. She sat down beside the fire to warm her hands. "I... don't want to go, given that Rolandus and I were planning on getting married, but if HaMelech has asked me to move, I will."

A hand settled on her shoulder and she looked up to see Rolandus. A sad smile played on his lips as he murmured, "I want you to listen to Him. We don't know when you need to leave, but we can at least enjoy time together before you do so." He kissed the top of her head and Marin nodded, leaning against his leg to watch the puppies eat.

Olare sighed. "What do we need to do to prepare you to go?"

"Wait for the next step." Marin looked at him. "I don't know when or why I'm leaving, and I don't want to go until I know what I need to do. Besides, I have Doves here who must learn how to care for chittering madness, and I don't think I can go before that is done."

Marin spent the next several weeks discussing with other Doves how to tend to chittering sickness and chittering madness.Herbs were planted, teas were made, and Marin spent her evenings scanning the shadows for demonic intruders. She would then pray in the unknown language, which she had begun to call her preyer tongue, to draw HaMelech's power to those spots.

All the while, she helped Rolandus tend to the pups that he was raising as they talked about the future and what their next step was. Rolandus smoothed her hair down. "I say we keep the engagement. We don't know how long it will be before you return, but... I want to be faithful to you. I promised you my heart, and I want to keep that promise."

"I can't hold you back, though," Marin murmured. She sighed. "You need to be able to wed-"

"I want you as my bride, Marin, and I'm willing to wait as long as it takes," Rolandus interrupted.

They shared a soft smile before Marin leaned against him and closed her eyes. "I love you."

"I love you too. It'll be alright, something will come of this and we'll still be okay."

They pressed their foreheads together and began to pray together quietly, finally embracing one another. Marin pressed her face into his shoulder, taking what comfort she could, before she pulled away and prepared for the rest of the day.

That afternoon, as Marin was finishing training the handful of Doves who were willing to help with chittering sickness, Sister Iren approached. "Marin, I'd like to go for a walk with you."

The younger woman paused, looked at Iren, and then brushed her hands on her apron. "Of course... we'll meet after having lunch. Please be certain to bring your notebooks and quills as we'll be going over tinctures that can speed up the recovery process. We'll also be working on harvesting the sprouted Valri plant." She watched the several healers disperse before she looked at Iren again. "It's been a while since we've walked together. The last time was when you were training me in midwifery. Is everything alright?"

Iren folded her hands before her, starting to walk towards the rose gardens. "Everything is just fine, better than, even. I'm pleased with what you've started on the chittering madness treatment, as well as your growth in following HaMelech. I overheard some of the others mentioning that you're praying in tongues, congratulations."

Marin's face grew hot. "Thank you, Sister Iren."

They walked quietly for a few minutes before Iren said, "I did want to discuss with you an opportunity for growth, and a potential... I wouldn't call it a promotion, but an opportunity to have extra responsibilities and a closeness to HaMelech."

"Oh?"

Iren stopped and faced Marin. "I wouldn't ask you to think of this without discerning, firstly, that you're meant to do this." Marin nodded and the older Dove continued, "We want to send someone to Zanther to serve those who are there. There are brothers and sisters who are there now, but they need help... especially as the Long Night approaches."

Marin shuddered at the reminder of the darkest 24 hours of the year, though she forced back her panic to ask, "Are you asking if I'd like to go?"

"I am, but as I said-"

"Then I will prepare for travel," Marin interrupted.

Sister Iren blinked at her. "Marin, this isn't a decision to take lightly. Rolandus and Olare would need to remain here in Apple Ridge, and you'd be able to communicate only through letters... and I know that you and Rolandus have entered marriage engagement-"

"I know, but this is something that HaMelech has laid on my heart, and I will be going as it is His will." Marin smiled a little bit. "Rolandus and I have already spoken about this, and we both know what steps I need to take."

Her mentor shifted. "...very well. We need to ensure that those you are leaving in your stead are fully trained to deal with chittering sickness. We're sending you out in two weeks' time, will that be possible for you to complete training then?"

"This is HaMelech's will, things will work out regardless."

Time flew by before Marin knew it. She celebrated her 21st birthday, completed training for the other Doves, prepared for her journey to Zanther, spent her evenings with Rolandus to savor the touch he could offer, and eventually, after a long goodbye, climbed into the caravan.

Rolandus stared up at her, his hand on her own. "I love you."

"I love you too. I promise I'll come back, okay?" Marin asked, smiling at him.

He returned the smile and they touched foreheads before he murmured, "I have something for you. You'll need to be careful wearing it, as it has the name of HaMelech on it, but... it's something for you to remember home with."

Marin held her hand out and he placed a delicate pendant in it. It was an apple, with tiny words engraved on the back:

Marin, chosen by HaMelech

Beloved by Rolandus

She stared at the necklace and then put it on, tucking it beneath her shawl. "Thank you. Please, be careful while I'm gone."

"Of course. Olare'll keep an eye on me, and I him." Rolandus kissed her forehead. "Write to me when you arrive."

"Of course, Rolandus."

Iren approached next, her hands folded in front of her. "Marin, you're certain that you'll be alright?"

"I'm positive."

The woman nodded before she murmured, "HaMelech has sent a message, and I believe it is for you. When you arrive, follow a woman with golden hair. I know that you've got contacts that you're staying with but... I don't know why HaMelech has this message, but hold fast to it."

"Golden hair?" Marin shifted as her mentor nodded, and then she murmured, "Alright... I'll follow a woman with golden hair and, if I can't find her, then I'll wait for my next steps."

Sister Iren left as the wagon lurched away, leaving Marin staring back as Rolandus waved at her. She wiped her face and waved to him before he disappeared from sight.

CHAPTER FIVE

First Night in Zanther

Marin carefully clutched her documents to her chest. They had worked tirelessly on them: a fake home, a false history of Solari worship, a work visa to support the story... all of it had been carefully crafted to help Marin enter Zanther with little questioning. In her pocket, nearly burning a hole through the fabric, was a roughcut piece of amber. As much as Marin hated carrying it, she knew the stone would validate her story- every Solari had one, as they needed it to speak to their 'god'.

It was a sad idea, needing a rock to pray, but Marin didn't voice that opinion. She was sure other Kingsmen felt the same, and the Solari knew no difference.

As she approached the outer wall of Zanther, Marin was taken aback by the sheer size of it. The wall itself was made of colossal ancient stones that towered over a hundred feet above her. There was no end in sight as it stretched in both directions for miles, almost big enough for her to believe in the old stories about the giants that once lived in this region.

The large gatehouse and courtyard that was built just outside of the wall was constructed out of newer stone and was much smaller by comparison. The first gate into the courtyard was easy to pass through, especially as only a single guard glanced at her. Marin was suddenly a part of a winding line of people moving through the courtyard and to the massive gates and booths before it. On either side of the courtyard, too, there was a statue and shrine. Each statue had a staff in one hand and a set of scales in the other: one had gold and goods on his scale while the other held kneeling people. Marin stared at the statutes, realizing they were the Solari gods Ireus and Drisis, the twin deities of travelers and merchants living and dead.

A small flock of round birds, similar to pigeons, pecked at some of the offerings that had been left behind. Their bulbous eyes moved independently from one another, one looking for acceptable crumbs while the other, comically, watched the crowd. "Shoo!" A pilgrim scolded, waving her cane. In an instant, the strange birds suddenly stood to reveal oddly large legs as they scattered with surprising speed. "Darn Zanther pigeons..."

Marin smiled slightly at the odd sight before she looked around, suddenly aware of a lingering dark presence around her. She looked around, watching as the black shadows washed over the area and swirled around people who passed by. Some seemed to have more of the darkness clinging to them, others seemed to simply move through like they were walking through a bog.

Amongst the people around her was a large, black, hulking figure. There was no real shape, only darkness, but its eyes had a dangerous glint to them. No one seemed to know it was there as it walked. Every so often, it stopped beside a person and plucked at their very being. Its victim sagged, life seeming to leave them, before it walked past them and moved to its next target. Only once did it look at Marin, but it then turned and walked away as though it wasn't interested in her.

The young woman stared after it before she was jostled from behind. "Move it! I want to see my grandson, and you're holding up the line!"

As quickly as the vision had appeared, it vanished.

Marin whispered a soft apology to the irate man behind her and approached the checkpoint. In the booth sat a bored looking guard. He was wearing Zanther colors, red with gold embellishment, and was currently playing with a piece of amber on a chain. The pilgrim before Marin provided her paperwork, answered a couple of questions, and then received a stamp on the topmost document. As the other woman walked away, the guard gestured for Marin.

She stepped forward, holding her documents ever tighter, and then placed them on the counter. The guard scanned the first page and then looked at Marin with one eyebrow raised. "Do you have a job here already?"

"Yes, sir. I was hired by a Mr. and Mrs. Jodius Rampart- she is a midwife in Zanther and I was going to work for her as I am trained in midwifery as well." Marin shifted, as the guard's eyes narrowed.

"I see. Where were you planning on staying?"

"Mr. and Mrs. Rampart had an empty space in their attic. Part of my employment was room and board," Marin said.

"Do you have proof of this?"

Marin nodded. "It's the third page in my documents, sir. I saved the letters we sent back and forth. Mrs. Rampart wrote to Godrick's Rest asking if we had any midwives available for hire as there was an influx of pregnancies in Zanther. We all wrote to her, and she selected me as her apprentice."

The guard skimmed the letter Marin was talking about before he sat the documents down. "Miss-" he glanced at her papers, "Lott, you are aware that Mr. and Mrs. Jodius Rampart were executed yesterday for practicing heresy and witchcraft, are you not?"

Marin's face ran cold and she slowly shook her head. "No, sir, I wasn't aware of that."

He frowned. "I see. Well, Miss Lott, as there seems to be no reason to be here-"

"Oi, Thaddius, get a load of this!"

Both Marin and the guard looked towards the shouting, where another guard had a young man by the scruff. "He's selling ambers... glass ambers!"

"No, sirs, you misunderstand! These are not meant for worship, simply... decoration!"

"Scoundrels... Let me finish this!" The guard before Marin fumbled for his stamp, knocking both over. He grabbed one, blindly, and then stamped Marin's top document. "Now, get out of here!" He all but tossed her papers to her. "Everyone, clear out! This gate check is now closed!" He hurried from his booth, leaving Marin to stare at her documents.

Approved.

"Thank HaMelech," she breathed, catching sight of the large 'rejected' stamp that remained abandoned on the table. With that, she pulled her cloak's hood up and hurried through the gate.

She didn't waste time looking for where to go. Instead, Marin flagged the first wagon she found. "Can you please take me to the inner wall?"

"It'll cost you."

Marin produced several small coins. "This is what I have to offer."

"Very well," the driver sighed.

Marin climbed amid his bags of flour and held onto the wagon as it lurched forward. Very few people looked towards them as they traveled through the hamlets between the walls, though Marin didn't focus on them. Instead, she watched as hulking shapes in the shadows walked around and plucked at the souls of Solari worshipers. Every so often,

Marin could see a person that the shadows avoided, but she didn't dare bring any attention to them.

It was dangerous. Her contacts had been found out, after all, even with all of the care they took. Now... Marin swallowed, trying to wrap her mind around what she could do.

There wasn't any place for her to go, nor was there a place to work. She was so preoccupied with her worries that she didn't realize the wagon stopped until the driver shook her. "Get going!"

The second checkpoint was easy compared to the first. They scanned her documents, found the approval stamp, and waved her through. Then, Marin stared around her to decide her next steps. The citadel before her made it difficult to focus: it was covered in brightly polished amber. Guards and inquisitors patrolled the streets, making people move to both sides of the road as they walked through. Marin stepped backwards and a group of guards got too close, but they didn't pay any attention to her.

Utterly lost, Marin began to walk the streets. Her stomach growled and she finally stopped. "Excuse me, I'm new to the city and I need something to eat. Where's the nearest-"

"Down the road and to the left," a little girl pointed, "it's got good food!"

Marin offered a weak smile and followed her directions. The little café was bursting at the seams, but Marin managed to find a seat after purchasing a small piece of bread and cheese to savor. She had just began to eat when a woman with brilliant blonde hair approached. "Hi! I know this is strange, but this is the only table left, and I don't have much time before returning to work. Can I sit with you?"

For a moment, Marin stared at her before she gave a little smile. "Sure."

The blonde sat across from her, beginning to ravenously eat. "Thank you! I wouldn't normally ask, but I won't be able to take another break until around 8 as I'm stuck in a double shift- you wouldn't believe how busy we've been! What with the inquisitors starting to crack down on Kingsmen worshipers, a lot of civilians have been injured in the crossfire and we're being worked to the bone. Top that with a lot of mothers expecting, and you get the picture."

As the woman spoke, Marin tilted her head. "You work at an infirmary?"

"The biggest and busiest in town... " The blonde began to chew on another bite, waving her fork. "Are you new to Zanther?"

Marin nodded slowly and then held her hand out. "I'm Marin Lott- I just made it past the walls today."

"I'm Anca Cassy. Sorry, normally I do what I can to introduce myself in a different way, but I don't have much time before Madame Justine will want me back... Wait a minute, how did you know I work at an infirmary?"

"Well... I've worked double shifts at an infirmary as well, and you're talking about midwifery issues and injuries..." Marin shifted, "I... guess it wasn't hard to figure out?"

Anca laughed, "I guess not, I'm a bit scatter-brained right now. Wait, you've worked double shifts before?" Anca stared at Marin before the bells of the citadel rang. She muttered under her breath, finished shoveling food in her mouth, and then stood. "Come on, we'll be late!"

"To what?"

"Work! Listen, I know that we haven't really met, but if you've worked as a healer before then we could really use your help... unless you already have a job. You don't have a job, do you?" Marin's silence made Anca beam and hold her hand out. "Then we'll get you one! I know that Justine will hire anyone who is competent, and this would be great for both of us. Please, will you come with me?"

Work? Go with her?

Marin stared at Anca before realizing that the sun had caught on the young woman's hair again. It was golden... like Iren had told her to look for. With that thought in mind, Marin took Anca's hand. "Lead the way, then. Will it cause issues in having my things with me?"

"We'll just tell Justine you're freshly from the wall. She won't care as long as you can tie a bandage."

Marin looked around. "Are you from Zanther, then?"

"Born and raised. My sister and I live a few blocks from here, I was heading to work when I ran into you," Anca answered. She smiled at Marin and, despite seeing the amber necklace that Anca wore, Marin smiled back.

Anca remained by her side as they entered the infirmary, which looked like it had been a warehouse at one point. Beds were neatly made and separated from one another. Marin also noticed some medical machines—similar to the ones they had in Apple Ridge, though much more expensive-looking — tucked into a closet.

"That's Catherine, there; she's one of the nurses who works here. She's been kind in showing me what to do to help others. Have you any training?"

Marin glanced at her. "I do, yes. That's what I was doing before I moved here. Mostly midwifery, but some more healing practices... nothing more than first aid."

She followed Anca through the building, realizing they had come through the back doors, and to the front foyer.

A simple desk had been set up, set out with two quills and a ledger. Behind the desk was a rather severe woman with a hawk-nose and glasses perched atop. Marin stiffened upon seeing the amber brooch prominently displayed. Her worries then spiked as the woman, Justine, looked at her. "You didn't come through the front doors."

"No, ma'am," Marin replied. She folded her hands in front of herself. "My name is Marin, I've just recently arrived in Zanther and was hoping to find work. Anca said that you needed additional healers here."

Justine hummed softly at her words, looked her over, and turned to her ledger. She didn't say anything as she thumbed through the back of the thick book. Marin shifted, cast a glance at Anca, and then looked at Justine as the older woman said, "Full name."

"Marin Lott."

"Full. Name."

"... Marin Marie Lott."

"Age."

"Just turned 21."

Justine glanced at her, raised an eyebrow, and went back to her book. "And where did you complete your training?"

"Midwifery and first aid were both completed in Godrick's Rest," Marin lied. "I started in Blackrock when I was very young and moved around since."

"I see... how many years have you been training?"

"On and off since I was 7, though it began more solidly when I turned 15."

Once more, Justine looked at her before she nodded. "Very well. Anca, you and Catherine will oversee her until she exits the probationary period. As for you, Marin, I'll lift restrictions in two months should you still be here. Now, off you get."

Marin released a breath as she turned, suddenly aware of how much panic had been rising in her chest. She glanced at Anca, who grinned, and then looked away. "I guess you'll introduce me to Catherine?"

"Of course!"

As Marin looked around, she allowed herself to study the darkness of the infirmary. There were some points of light as she looked around: many had settled around people who were tending to injured or sick.

A majority of the individuals, though, had darkness simply clinging to them. Anca was one of them— while she didn't have any creatures latched onto her, Marin could see that the shadows were pulling away at her very core.

They approached Catherine, a woman with tired eyes, and Anca introduced them. Marin was too heavily focused on the other woman to say much. She was surprised to see light shining from this woman, a light that made even the demons on Anca shy away.

There was no doubt that Catherine was a Kingsman, too.

"Marin, are you alright?"

"I'm sorry, I was thinking about something," Marin replied. She took Catherine's extended hand and shook it. "It's nice to meet you."

"And you as well. Anca said you're new to Zanther?"

"I am," Marin said. As she watched Catherine and then looked at Anca, she remembered Sister Iren's message. Anca had led her to her next step.

Anca beamed at them. "You two chat while I get more bottles. Oh, this is so exciting!" She ran off, leaving the two alone.

Marin settled beside Catherine as the woman began to work on bottling tinctures. "Catherine?"

"Yes?"

"I'm like you."

Catherine paused, glanced at Marin out of the corner of her eye, and returned to bottling. "Oh?"

"I follow HaMelech, too," Marin breathed.

Catherine stopped again, looking at Marin. The exhaustion in her eyes changed to that of concern as she whispered, "Why hadn't I received a letter?"

"Well... you weren't my contact. I was supposed to be with the Ramparts-"

"Oh... oh, I'm so sorry to tell you but they're gone now," Catherine murmured. She shook her head. "The inquisitors found them two days ago."

"I know, so... I think you're my next step. Anca brought me here, and she was the person I was supposed to follow."

Catherine frowned and opened her mouth before Anca returned to their side. As soon as the blonde appeared, Marin glanced at her. "Is there anything I should know?"

Anca nodded. "We pray to Solaris three times a day, plus meals. You missed our first prayer, but we'll have another one at 1 and then a third at 5 before we leave. Anyone who is here overnight will pray at different points, but you'll be here from 9 to 5 with us."

"It's a moment of silence and petition," Catherine included, "Not verbal." Marin nodded, relaxing in the presence of the older woman, as Anca began to explain the routines.

As the noon meal came to be, Marin sat beside Catherine and Anca. There, they each bowed their heads. Anca grasped a delicate amber necklace and Catherine clutched at something on the end of a golden chain. The older of the three glanced at Marin, who grabbed the piece of amber from her pocket again.

Bile rose in her chest and Marin, as softly as she could, began to pray, "King of Kings... remove the darkness. Flood us with Your light, redeem us."

Footsteps paused behind her and Marin sucked in a breath, "Thank you for Your provisions, thank you for Your mercy."

It seemed to appease whomever it was who walked behind her, as no one spoke.

Marin spared a look at Catherine, who sighed as well. They began to eat after that point, listening to Anca before the youngest of the group paused. "Marin?"

"Yes?"

"Why did you decide to come to Zanther if you were Godrick's Rest? Isn't Blackrock closer?"

The question made Marin stop, thinking over her answer. "Blackrock was closer, but I needed to come here. I don't know why, but I didn't want to disobey what I felt."

Anca nodded and Catherine murmured, "Sometimes, all you can do is listen."

"Are you going to miss Godrick's Rest?" Anca asked.

Again, Marin paused. Finally, she murmured, "Not so much the place, but the people. I left behind my brother and a very dear friend. I was meant to get married to him before I came here."

Catherine rested a hand on her arm and Marin offered a little smile. "He wanted me to come. We knew that we'd separate for a time, but... I trust him, and he trusts me."

The women fell silent for a moment before Anca murmured, "I hope you can see him again. My sister, Adriata, says that there's no true thing as love; she's been hurt many times even before she started working at the brothel. I like to think that there's someone out there, waiting for each of us but..." she trailed off, "Solaris has other plans depending on faithfulness." She offered a forced smile before she finished her food. "I suppose we should get back to patients."

"Yes, let's." Catherine stood, and then paused, looking at Marin. She studied the red-haired woman, enough that Marin shifted, before she murmured, "There is a plan for you here. I will walk with you home this evening, and we will speak privately."

"I haven't currently got a place to stay-"

"Then I will walk with you to my home, and you can stay with us until you do find one."

After a long day, they were released, and Marin walked beside Catherine. Anca had gone the other direction, allowing them to speak in hushed tones as they avoided crowds. "Are you really from Godrick's Rest?"

"Apple Ridge. I am a Dove healer who did spend time in Godrick's Rest, but that was for training," Marin whispered, "I met a woman there who taught me how to take care of chittering sickness. As for why exactly I'm here," she paused as a group of inquisitors passed, keeping her eyes on the ground until they were gone, "I'm uncertain."

Catherine nodded, looping her arm with the other woman. "Well, welcome to Zanther. It's not the nicest city, but you'll be okay. Did anyone else come with you from Apple Ridge?"

Marin shook her head, "Just me." They paused at a little house nestled amongst larger buildings. A little girl was playing outside with some of her dolls and her head perked up as soon as she saw them.

"Mamma!"

Her shock of red hair made Marin smile, especially as the child flung her arms around Catherine. Catherine smoothed her hair, kissed her forehead, and glanced at Marin, "Annabell, this is Marin. Marin, this is my daughter Annabell." Marin gave a brief greeting before they hurried inside with Annabell and locked the door.

A handful of oil lamps were burning, shedding light alongside the fireplace. Marin looked around, homesickness hitting her. "You have a lovely home."

"It's not much, but it's cozy," Catherine said. She directed Marin to a seat. "Now... you are from Apple Ridge, and they don't care about the High Inquisitors do they?" Marin shook her head and Catherine sighed. "Alright, that's a lot for you to learn to remain safe here." Marin blinked at her as Catherine murmured, "With the High Inquisitors... the council is beginning to grow stricter in looking for Kingsmen. More guards are patrolling, more inquisitors, than before. This isn't the time for mistakes."

Marin said, "My brother did his best to prepare me; he's served with the Bleak Hollow Brigade and knows that everyone is required to attend worship and that there are... eight... who are High Inquisitors."

"That's at least something." Catherine nodded and then glanced at Annabell. The little girl had returned to playing with her dolls, this time inside with them. For a moment, neither adult spoke before Catherine whispered, "They don't tell you how dangerous it is here until you've arrived. It's a witch hunt, and we are guilty regardless of what we do. The High Inquisitors rule with an iron fist. Sure, they have their priests and the high priest, but they're puppets more than anything. High Inquisitor Treatis is the oldest and has been in power for nearly 40 years. Alastar is next, at 30, as he started very young; he has a son somewhere in the city. My husband, James, is certain that he must be serving as an inquisitor and is being groomed to take a position in the council once something happens. As of currently, it's merely rumors."

She continued to name the High Inquisitors- Lillian, Greaves, Langston, Belleville, Saville, and Lynch- before she murmured, "HaMelech is higher than any of them, and I trust His plan. My only prayer is that we do not enter the fold as martyrs... not now."

"What about Anca?"

"What about her?"

Marin shifted. "She's Solari, but... there's something different. Looking at her, the creatures clinging to her seem to be trying harder to stay."

Catherine tilted her head before realization flooded her gaze, "You can see into the spirit realm, can't you?" Marin's nod made her laugh, "HaMelech promised I would meet someone who could do that. That is why you were comfortable speaking to me about HaMelech when we first met, then?"

"You don't have darkness holding onto you." Marin rubbed the back of her neck.

The other Kingsman smiled and stood. "I pray that your faithfulness only grows stronger in the future. I do need to begin making dinner-"

"May I help?"

The sudden question made Catherine blink. Marin stood, shifting. "I'd make dinner nightly with my older brother, and I'd like to do something with a friend. I'm homesick, I can't lie, and this... this is something I know that I miss from Apple Ridge."

"Then please, come help me."

They began to peel potatoes and chop vegetables as Catherine said, "Anca is a sweet girl, but she is Solari. But... I've noticed that she doesn't seem to be so tightly bound to their beliefs as others, such as Justine. I'm not sure if she truly believes in Solaris or if she's walking on a path that she knows exists since she has no other path to step onto."

"How do we go about telling her about HaMelech, then?"

Marin's newfound friend glanced at her, sadness spreading through her face. "We might not ever be able to, Marin. With the others that we work with, we need to be ever mindful as we could be found out."

"She deserves to know who HaMelech is, though, as we're His daughters."

"I know, but with the inquisitors... the last thing I want is for her to find HaMelech and then a pyre."

Marin paused in chopping a carrot. "Catherine, it isn't fair."

Catherine sighed, "You'll understand one day, Marin."

They returned to making dinner in silence, though Marin couldn't help but think about Anca. She offered a silent prayer to HaMelech, thanking Him for showing her the next steps and giving her a chance to meet Catherine, when the door opened and Catherine whipped around, brandishing her kitchen knife.

Her fears were quelled as a tall man with red hair stepped in, his face tired though his eyes shone with a life akin to Catherine's.

"James, you scared us!"

"I'm sorry, dear: work got off early and I decided to come straight home." He set his hat on a hook and hung up his coat as well before he glanced at Marin. "You must be a friend of Catherine's?"

"I'm Marin, one of the new healers at the infirmary."

"Well, welcome to our home." James gestured around before Annabell raced into his arms. They embraced and she pulled him into one of the back rooms where his laugh echoed from.

Catherine sighed, smiling after him. "He's a good man."

"He seems it," Marin murmured. As she watched Catherine, she couldn't help but feel jealousy and anger rise in her chest. There was nothing fair in having left Rolandus, or her brother, in Apple Ridge. The happy couple was a bitter reminder of what she had lost.

Marin grasped the pendant around her neck, doing her best to focus on obeying HaMelech in following the path to Zanther, but it did little as Catherine looked at her. "Are you alright?"

"No." Marin looked away from Catherine. It took no more than a moment before Catherine gave a quiet sound and rested her hand on Marin's back. The younger of the two shifted, "It's okay. I knew things like this would come up and..." She looked down. "I miss Rolandus, and I miss my brother Olare."

"I'm sorry, Marin. Maybe you'll go home soon?"

"Not until HaMelech releases me from this call," Marin murmured.

Later that evening, Marin watched as James began to work on transcribing the Holy Text into a second book. He explained that his call was to ensure those in Zanther had a copy they could read. Marin watched in fascination as he copied some letters and then showed her a small printing press. Painstakingly, he placed rows of lettered blocks together and then rolled ink over them. As soon as he had, he pressed a sheet of paper to the ink and then after several moments, produced a single page. "It's a long process, but it has brought the Word to many others."

After a long night, Marin left for the infirmary with Catherine the next morning. Once she saw Anca, though, she had a feeling that she needed to focus on her during the day.

The young blonde had her hair piled atop her head in a knot and was wearing a grey gown today. Marin looked herself over, her cheeks growing hot as she realized there were so many other options that she could have worn, and then sighed.

In an instant, Anca was by her side. Marin braced herself for questioning but instead found herself wrapped in the other's embrace. "G ood... morning!"

"Good morning! Was your first night in Zanther okay?" Anca asked. She pulled away and grinned, a smile so infectious that Marin began to beam as well.

She liked Anca. While she had things she was dealing with, it was clear that she genuinely loved and cared for those whom she met. Marin nodded at her question. "It was alright."

"Good! If you ever need, my sister Adriata and I have extra rooms in our home. It isn't much, but it's more than nothing." Anca took Marin's hand, beginning to lead her back to where patients lay in their beds. "Catherine was sent for earlier today. I think Justine has a special assignment for her... she's always liked Catherine." She shook her head. "I was hoping that she'd show me how to better do sutures: I've got the basic knot down, but I want to know if there's more or better options."

After looking around to find that Catherine had already left , Marin murmured, "I can give you some insight if you'd like. While surgery isn't my main focus, I know quite a few sutures that can be used. I've got my preference for stitching small wounds, you might want to know those."

Her newfound friend nodded, grasped her hand again, and pulled her into the infirmary. The rest of the day, Marin showed Anca a variety of stitches she knew. The younger of the two stared in awe and copied it on her small patch of practice muslin. After a moment, Anca said, "You don't want to be in Zanther, do you?"

"Why do you say that?"

"You don't seem very happy."

Marin looked back at her stitches, her voice growing quiet, "I'm having a hard time being here."

Anca stopped what she was doing, frowning. "I'm sorry, Marin. Is it because you miss the young man you were talking about yesterday, or something more?"

The question was innocent, but it stabbed Marin deeper than she thought it would. She stared at Anca, suddenly realizing that tears were beginning to sting her eyes. "It's that and other things. I know I miss Rolandus deeply, but I'm trying to avoid thinking about him. It's done nothing but cause me pain as of late, even though I know he still loves me and I love him."

Anca took her hand and gave it a soft squeeze. "Maybe he'll follow you here."

"It isn't his place to come to Zanther, not at this point," Marin murmured.

Within an instant, Anca wrapped her arms around Marin and held her tightly. It took a moment before Marin relaxed in Anca's arms and pressed her face into her shoulder. Anca sighed, "I'm sorry, Marin. I don't know what it's like, but I can only imagine how hard it is."

Marin nodded and pulled away. "I'd like to get things finished for the day, please."

After several hours, Catherine returned. They didn't speak much as Anca was busy showing Marin different procedures, and eventually they were released to go home. Catherine walked with Marin, remaining rather silent about the special task it was she had undertaken. She was brief in stating that it was, in fact, a specific duty from Justine, but aside from that she said nothing more. Instead, she focused on asking

Marin questions about Apple Ridge, the people she knew, and what she was hoping to do while in Zanther. When they sat to eat, Marin was surprised to see there was a letter addressed to her. James explained that it had been sent to one of the Kingsmen contacts in the city and, through the grapevine, he was able to get it for her.

Marin read it quietly, doing her best to keep from crying. Rolandus had sent it, and in the letter he explained that the chittering sickness was growing bad again. He assured her that he was going to be alright as she did train the others, and that he was proud of her. Marin stared at it, suddenly growing aware that it had been opened and resealed, before she folded it and placed it beside her plate again. She didn't tell her hosts what had been said, and slipped quietly to her room after she ate.

All around her, she could see shadows beginning to creep towards her to choke her out. She shut her eyes tighter, took a breath, and whispered, "Why am I here?" Silence answered as she breathed, "I am not qualified for this, HaMelech. I want to be home, I want to be building a life with Rolandus, and… and I want to be safe. This isn't a safe place."

Marin opened her eyes, realizing as she did that the shadows had begun to swarm over her. She hadn't noticed it before, but as they clung to her she grew aware of stinging pain radiating over her and a whisper in her ear, "Just go home."

The voices clambered over one another, each telling her to go home or that she was unworthy. In a final roar, Marin began to sob as one voice rang out, "You are worthless!"

She clung to herself, trying to ignore the accusations and anxiety that began to eat at her, before she finally managed, "HaMelech help me."

The fear and pain didn't leave her and Marin, without anything else to do, laid down. She continued to cry for what felt like hours before the softest whisper of, *"You need to stay."*

A quiet knock sounded on the door and Marin, after a moment, asked who it was.

Catherine came in, paused, and then shut the door. She sat beside Marin. "Are you alright?"

Marin stared at Catherine, tears beginning to fill her eyes again. Finally, she managed, "I don't want to be here, I don't want to do what He's called me to but... but I have to obey. I have to do as He says because His is my God. I'm so angry, and frustrated, and I don't know what to do, and I hate it!" She broke down, sobbing. Catherine didn't say a word and Marin said, "I feel like I've had every hope and dream I held onto pull from me. I lost the life I was expecting to live, I've been called to this city where my life is constantly on the line, and... and I feel so alone and like the only thing I can do is move forward because He told me to! Rolandus is getting worse, the letter he sent was opened by someone and... and I can't even do anything to help him!"

Her friend remained silent before she shifted closer and held her arms out. Marin leaned into her, crying into her chest. She couldn't breathe through her sobs, making her shudder as she did suck in air, and finally she laid limp in Catherine's arms.

Still, Catherine said nothing.

Finally, the older woman whispered, "If HaMelech had left you to suffer this walk alone, then He would not be the mighty God we know. If He abandoned you after calling you to this city to serve in a way that we don't understand, then He is nothing more than one of the Solari gods that our lost friends follow. HaMelech has never abandoned you, and He never will. He's carried you this far, and I can see it: He gifted you with a patience to work with the seriously ill, those who have chittering madness, and those who are lost. Rolandus is still a gift HaMelech sent you. He has not pulled you to a place where no one cares about you, as He brought you into my life and the lives of those you serve with. Your orders to move are to allow you to walk beside Him, as it is the suffering of this journey that shows us where His strength carries us. He is holding you now, Marin, as I know none of this would be possible if He was not with you."

Marin shook her head. "Then why isn't He doing anything?"

"He is, you know He is. You are under such severe attack, Marin, and I'm so sorry. Can we pray together? Can I pray for you?"

Marin nodded and Catherine held her tighter. She was silent for a moment, and then whispered, "HaMelech, we are so thankful for the gifts you've provided, even when we are frightened and confused. We know that you did not create us to have a spirit of fear, and yet the world does what it can to make us afraid. Inquisitors, threat of capture... none of these things come from you, and we know this, but we also know that You have everything under Your control and that Your will is perfect. You are perfect. Thank you for sending Marin here and her obedience to what you have called her- You have instilled such a gentle faithfulness in her and have so gracefully broken the bindings that she has on her life. We know that you have control over every aspect of her life and that you are protecting everyone she loves in Apple Ridge. Thank you for being a good God and a good Father. We love You and are so grateful for each of the precious gifts you have given us."

Catherine's voice faded to a whisper as she began to whisper in a foreign tongue. Marin wasn't sure what she was saying, but the soft words brought her comfort and peace. Before she knew it, she had fallen asleep.

CHAPTER SIX

Finding Her Place

Most of Marin's time with the Conroys was attending worship together in secret. The first meeting brought more tears than not as they prayed for Marin, asking for guidance and wisdom in this unknown calling. In the later meetings, Marin explained to the gathered assembly that she trained in treating chittering sickness. That brought many questions and prayers, and Marin had more people whom she was seeing daily to offer prayer and comfort as they struggled.

Two weeks after arriving in Zanther, she found Catherine packing a small bag of food. "What are you doing?"

"Preparing for the Long Night. I'll be serving with the other Doves outside of our home."

"I need to do something, too," Marin said.

Catherine glanced at her. "You know how dangerous it is to be in Zanther during the Long Night... as a Kingsman, right?"

Marin shifted. "Yes, but I also know that HaMelech gave me the knowledge and ability for a time like this. I have yet to help you or anyone else know what to do when dealing with chittering madness outside of prayer and rest, and if I can be of use then I need to be. I'll stay in one of our places of worship, simply bring people to me."

"It's 24 hours of darkness... people fall to their desires and it isn't safe."

Marin crossed her arms. "I guess I should move into a Solari city in the middle of a witch hunt- that should be safer than the Long Night. Look, HaMelech guides me and His will is greater than the darkness that surrounds us. Now... what can I do to help?

Her friend stared at her before she sighed and nodded. "Alright. We'll get you set up in one of the churches to serve against chittering madness."

The two slipped from their home and hurried down the street, shrouded in the darkness of night. There wasn't much time to prepare before the Eye of the Dragon, a black orb, would hang in the sky and signal the Long Night. As Marin and Catherine set up in one of the underground churches, they were joined by six other Dove healers, seven Kingsmen who did not serve, and a knight. Marin frowned as they entered and Catherine explained, "They have had chittering madness in the past."

"It gets worse during the Long Night," a young man said quietly, "Being together, with other Kingsmen, is the only way to make it better but... it only helps so much."

Marin nodded a little at his explanation and then glanced at Catherine. "What do you want me to do?"

"Get comfortable," the knight said in Catherine's stead. "If anything happens, we'll need to be well rested."

Again, Marin nodded before she went about getting herself ready. Each of the Doves sat beside someone who had been infected and Marin, seeing one of the others was seated beside the knight, joined her. The knight glanced at her. "What are you doing?"

"You've got the worst of the flareups, don't you?" Marin asked, ignoring the knight. The young woman before her nodded and Marin smiled. "It'll be okay. One of my dear friends back home had severe chittering sickness, and it would manifest. He's doing much better now, I know you'll do alright, too." Her words seemed to calm the young woman and Marin took her hands as the howling of the monsters outside grew. The knight beside them rested his hand on the hilt of his sword and Marin murmured, "It's going to be okay. HaMelech is mightier than the darkness." She pulled the woman beside her close and then pulled a handful of dried Valri petals from one of her pouches. "Try this, it'll help soothe you."

The woman nodded and ate the petals, her body growing lax. Marin stroked her hair, watching her, before she murmured, "Try and sleep. I am here, keeping watch, and rest will do you good."

As the woman turned into Marin's side, Marin began to pray over her, "HaMelech, thank you for your mercy and your love. We cannot comprehend how You, the great healer, can knit together broken bodies and minds the way You do. Thank you for keeping us close, and thank you for healing where our abilities fail us. You truly are the One King, maker and keeper of this world and of us. We bow before You tonight, knowing that You ultimately have defeated the Black Dragon and that we will rejoice yet again under the sun. Until then, we whisper our quiet praise and adoration as You protect us from the dangers around us." Finally, she murmured, "Get some rest, all of you. I know it's frightening, but we cannot forget who it is that lights our paths and makes them straight before Him."

The others fell asleep, too, after some hot tea that the knight brewed for them and a few of the petals Marin offered. She helped each get comfortable before she glanced at Catherine. "We still need to pray over them while they rest. Now is the time that HaMelech can truly work, as we are not impeding Him with our overactive minds."

Catherine nodded at her and the small group of Doves began to pray over their sleeping charges.

As the Long Night dragged on, one of the Doves began to sing praises to HaMelech. Others would join, then another would lead, before another and then another would start the song over. Marin could see the dark shadows at the door, begging to come in but unable to cross the threshold. After many hours of singing, one of the other Doves approached Marin. "Water?"

"Thank you," Marin murmured, taking a long drink.

"Sister Ulma is preparing food as it's around what should be midday. Can you help her pass them out to our charges?"

Many hours later, Marin struggled to remain awake. Working double shifts had nothing on trying to remain awake and alert in such a small room, especially where there was not much happening. There had been one chitter scare that the knight had put down, but aside from that their prayers seemed to keep the worst of it at bay. When dawn finally came, and the sun returned, Marin yawned. The woman who had rested beside Marin embraced her tightly. "HaMelech keep you, dear child. He has such a beautiful plan for you!"

"Thank you, really," Marin said. She smiled at the woman, closed her eyes as the soft prayers and thanksgivings lifted to HeMelech, and rested until they were able to slip home.

After five months of living with the Conroys, Marin shifted as she meditated over the Holy Texts. There was something there, asking her to listen to the nearly silent voice that whispered to her. Marin took a deep breath and stilled, allowing herself to lean into the silence. As she did, the gentlest thought crossed her mind, prompting her to find a way to spend more time with Anca.

Marin furrowed her brow, trying to coax anything more from the Breath of HaMelech who she knew was speaking to her, but she was unable to do so. Rather than growing frustrated, she instead remained in prayer longer as she murmured her quiet questions, praises, and petitions.

When she finished, Marin dusted herself off and left to find Catherine. Her friend was in the kitchen, kneading a thick bread dough before it was to go into a pot to bake in the fire. Marin shifted. "Catherine?"

"Yes?"

"I think I need to move out."

Catherine glanced at her, one floured hand on her hip. "That's a strange thought. Is there something wrong?"

"No, nothing's wrong," Marin said. She pushed some hair from her face, beginning to knead the dough as Catherine shifted over. "I was praying and I got the feeling that I need to spend more time with Anca. I'm not entirely sure why I need to move, but... I do."

Her friend gave a little hum, lost in thought, before she nodded. "If this is HaMelech moving, we're not going to stand in your way."

Catherine embraced her and Marin closed her eyes. "I appreciate everything, Catherine."

"You're speaking as though you won't see us again," Catherine murmured, laughing, "That's not going to happen, you know this."

"I know, I know."

Marin attended her shift at the infirmary alone that day. Halfway down the street, she paused at a house. From inside, she could hear soft crying and a hushed voice begging for someone to snap out of some sort of stupor. Marin paused, chewed on her lip, and then knocked on the door.

A timid-looking man opened it a crack. "What do you want?"

"Is everyone okay in there?" Marin asked.

The man nodded before a low moan came from within the house. Marin frowned, "I'm a healer, is there anything I can do?"

"N-no! No, nothing's wrong..." He trailed off, looked at Marin, and then whispered, "Are you with the inquisitors?"

"No, I'm not."

Snatching her hand, he pulled her into his home before she could even speak. The door slammed shut, and Marin spun around, reay to defend herself, until she noticed something in the corner.

It was a frail woman, curled into a ball with blankets around her. As Marin stared at her, she became aware of the shadows that clung to her and threatened to swallow her whole. Marin glanced at the man. "How long has she had chittering madness?"

"N-no, don't say that word!" The man said, waving his hands, "She's fine, she is... she's ..."

"What's her name?" Marin asked.

"... Isla. Please, you said you're a healer." He wrung his hands. "Can you help her?"

Marin looked at him, then at Isla, and then nodded. "I can help soothe the symptoms at the very least. How long has she been like this?"

"Three days. One of those monsters appeared in an alleyway and..."

Isla didn't move until Marin crouched beside her, her eyes frantic. "I see them... help me, they want to consume me!"

Marin shook her head. "It's alright, Isla, they won't hurt you. Can you tell me what your husband's name is?"

"B-Beret."

"Okay. Beret, please begin to boil water for Isla to have some tea and bone broth. Come here, my dear." Marin took Isla into her arms. "It's time to rest: you're safe now, your husband is here, and the monsters cannot harm you." She helped the woman to her bed and tucked her in, resting one hand on her forehead. Marin took a deep breath, mentally praying to HaMelech for protection before she closed her eyes and began to whisper a prayer over Isla. She could feel Beret watching, the hair rising on the back of her neck before she realized that Isla had fallen asleep during the prayer. The shadows around her were fading, slowly, and Marin brushed hair from her face.

Beret approached. "What did you do? What did you do to help my Isla?"

Marin glanced at him. "I..." she trailed off and shifted.

If she said she was following HaMelech, there was a high chance that she'd be arrested.

Finally, after a moment of silence, Marin said, "I am praying to my lord, HaMelech, the true King of Kings." She stared at Beret, blinking before the man knelt beside the bed and took Isla's hand.

"Solaris... he is the true god."

Marin took a deep breath and then rested her hand on Beret's shoulder. "Solaris only has enough power as you believe he does. HaMelech truly has power. He can heal, He can save... His hand rests on Isla now as she sleeps. Has Solaris done anything to bring her peace, let alone healing?"

Beret didn't answer and Marin turned back to Isla. "HaMelech is king and has power over the darkness." She stared at Isla, doubt beginning to creep into the back of her mind. What if this wasn't from HaMelech and it was just her wishing for a miracle? No, she needed to trust. Marin took a deep breath, "In the name of HaMelech, I command you to depart from Isla, and for her health to be restored. You have no power here, as this is the domain of my Lord and Savior." In an instant, the sweat beading from Isla's brow cleared and she fell into a natural, deep sleep.

Marin stared at the woman, her eyes wide in amazement, before she whispered, "Thank you HaMelech for hearing our cries. Thank you for healing her, thank you for letting me see this miracle..."

As Marin prayed, she realized that Beret was sobbing beside her. She glanced at him before she looked at Isla and then whispered, "HaMelech is a kind God, and He loves all: you merely need to come home."

"How?"

His question surprised Marin and she paused before she said, "Turn away from the false god Solaris and welcome HaMelech into your heart. Nothing more is needed aside from the desire to let Him into your life."

The man was trembling as he nodded and Marin, without thinking about it, took his hand and held it. "Alright... if you're certain, we'll pray right now, okay?"

"O-okay."

"Father HaMelech, thank you for the safety we have in this home..."

Marin ran to the infirmary as soon as she was through helping the newfound Kingsmen, out of breath as she hurried through the doors. Justine glanced towards her. "You're late."

"I stopped to help someone along the way."

"Hm. Fine, write it in your report."

Marin nodded and then raced to where she had been keeping her ledger. As she was calming down, Anca approached. "Marin! There you are! Catherine said you left home an hour ago-"

"I had to take care of something on the way, I'm sorry," Marin murmured. She glanced at Anca and then paused. "Where is Catherine?"

"She went to run an errand." Anca began to help her fold bandages. "I'm surprised you were here after her."

"I was late, I didn't mean to be. I was lost in thought thinking about where I might be moving to and then I was distracted by a... house call. I feel bad: I don't want to be a burden for the Conroy's while I look-"

"You're moving?"

"Yes, but it's not because of Catherine or her family. I just... feel like it's time to move."

"Do you want to stay with Adriata and I?"

Marin blinked before she nodded. "That would be really nice. It won't be for long, just until I find a new place."

Anca leaned against her before she returned to what she was doing. Marin smiled and turned her attention back to the bandages. Catherine came in an hour later with Anabell in tow. Marin gave the little girl a tight hug and looked up at Catherine. "I thought you would have been here sooner."

"We were, but Justine needed us to run a medicinal tea to one of the High Inquisitors. There's a horrible cough running through Zanther, one that's causing some pretty severe symptoms on top of it," Catherine explained. She pulled her bonnet off and placed it on the hook. After a moment, she murmured, "High Inquisitor Treatis is older, and his lungs are strained due to it."

"May Solaris heal him," Anca mumbled.

Marin glanced briefly at her before turning her gaze to Catherine. The older brunette shrugged and put a hand on Anabell's shoulder. "Let's get you washed, my love, and I'll have you help me make herbal capsules. Marin, can you and Anca work on bottling tinctures and give the daily doses to each of our patients?"

The four separated and Marin began to do as she was asked, though she kept an eye on Anca. Her blonde friend had turned away from them but, as Marin watched her, she became aware of Anca's avoidance of Justine and the other Solari. The shadows around Anca were swirling in a different way before, making Marin frown before she returned to what she was doing.

When it came time for the midday meal, Anca had disappeared. Marin ate beside Catherine in disciplined silence, listening to Annabell tell her about school as she spoke between mouthfuls before they returned to their tasks.

Anca still hadn't returned then.

It wasn't until Marin had pulled her walking coat on and had started to leave that Anca reappeared, her eyes exhausted and hair in disarray.

She tied her hat to her head, fixed her hatpin, and then glanced at Marin. "Oh. You're still here."

"I am... are you alright?"

"I... will be. Had a run-in with inquisitors as I was running an errand; they selected me for random questioning. I guess they thought I looked suspicious and they interrogated me. Justine wrote off the hours." Anca brushed a strand of hair from her eyes. "Where are you staying tonight?"

Marin frowned, linked her arm with Anca, and began to walk with her to the door. "I was going to stay with you, remember? You look awful, though. I can find a different place to rest over the night-"

"No, no, you can come home with me." Her younger friend smiled, patting her hand. "It's just been a long day."

The two slipped from the infirmary and made their way down the street, chatting idly about the day. All the while, Marin kept a keen eye out for any patrolling guards or inquisitors that might move towards them. There were none, and she soon found herself standing before a small home towards the edge of the city.

Anca opened the door and then paused. "My sister, Adriata, is intimidating at first but she's a good person. Just... please don't be surprised when you first meet her. We had to make a living somehow before I started to work."

Marin raised an eyebrow and followed Anca inside.

It was a simple home, but it was decorated more than Catherine's. A portrait hung above the fireplace of Anca and a woman who looked like her. As Marin stared at it, she became aware of someone watching her in return. She turned to see the other woman from the portrait, a tall woman with stern eyes and straight blonde hair. She was wearing a dressing robe, one that opened most of the way, and was holding a cup of coffee in her hand. Traces of makeup stained beneath her eyes and made her look more tired than she was. Marin straightened up. "Hello, you must be-"

"Solaris keep you," the woman interrupted, lifting a hand, "You must be one of Anca's friends... Marin?"

"So she's told you about me?"

"All good things, I suppose. I'm her sister, Adriata." She settled into a chaise, sipped her coffee, and glanced at Anca. "I thought you were going to offer that she stays with us and then come with her the next day, Anca."

Anca shrugged, gestured for Marin to sit, and then sat beside her. "Well, things change, Adriata. On that note, patrols are growing more frequent."

Marin glanced at Adriata, who had narrowed her eyes. As she studied the woman, the amount of darkness that covered her nearly consumed everything in the room. It was only strengthened as Adriata said, "Good: then they'll be able to find those who bring curses upon this city. The 'Kingsmen' must be given a new opportunity in life... may Solaris grant them mercy in their rebirth."

"Something will come of it," Anca said. They sat in silence for a moment before Anca asked, "Are you working tonight?"

"I have a shift in a couple of hours, just woke up," Adriata answered. She glanced at Marin. "I assume you're still working with Anca?" Marin nodded and Adriata stood. "Good. You'll need to pay us at least a part of the rent, especially when we're buying food so that we can all eat."

She left before Marin was able to respond and Anca, after she did, murmured, "She does have a good heart, though she seems to be less than kind. I'll show you to your room, you're probably tired after your day."

"I'm sure you are, too."

The two slowly moved through the home to a little bedroom. It had nothing more than a bed, though Anca reassured Marin that they could put in a writing desk in one of the common rooms if she wanted to so she could write home. Marin took her up on the offer, wrote a letter to the postmaster to have mail delivered to the Cassy's home until further notice, and then rested.

Life was unchanged as she stayed with Anca and Adriata, though it grew more and more difficult to attend her worship and not Solari worship. When she was with the Conroys, she was able to avoid going to the Solari services twice a week. They merely remained home, silent and with unlit lights. Now, living with two Solari women meant that she had to attend.

Marin walked arm in arm with Anca as they made their way to the Solari temple. Adriata was in front of them, her head held up proudly as the sun glinted off of her amber necklace. Anca was more reserved, her head covered with a bonnet as though to keep the inquisitors at the doors from recognizing her. Marin avoided their shrouded faces as well, holding onto Anca tighter before she found herself staring at a dais and a pulpit.

She did her best to ignore the man speaking as the shadows around her threatened to consume all around her. There were points of light throughout the assembly, though they were few and far between. There were more dark ethereals walking between people and absorbing them than she saw before. It wasn't until the end of the service, where a line of prisoners were marched from one door and to the pyre and stakes that had been erected, that Marin's mouth went dry.

Each had the hood over their head removed, their crimes read, and were hung from the pole. All were Kingsmen, given the verdict of death for following HaMelech, and they hung there until the last crime was read. Then, the inquisitors who had led them out plunged their flaming swords into the pyre to light it.

If this hadn't made Marin sick to her stomach, hearing the cheers of the Solari worshipers would have.

None of them spoke as they returned home, and Marin sat down as Adriata commented, "It's been a while since we've had an execution like that. The inquisitors must be doing a better job at finding the heretics."

"Mhm," Anca murmured. She focused on the embroidery in her lap. "I can't help but wonder how their families are feeling after this, though."

"Why does it matter? They will be reborn into faithful Solari worshipers again. Worst case scenario they are curseborn, but even that it better than being a heretic. You might as well have your soul consumed by the Black Dragon at that point." Adriata leaned back on her chaise, beginning to sip at a small glass of brandy, and then paused. "What did you think, Marin? We haven't had an execution like that since before you came here."

"We didn't have executions like that in Godrick's Rest, or anywhere else I stayed," Marin said. She shifted a bit, "It was overwhelming, to say the least."

Adriata shrugged. "There'll be plenty of time to grow accustomed to it. If they found one nest of the heretics, they'll find another soon enough. The inquisitors are well known for getting information as needed."

Marin nodded, weakly, and then murmured, "I see. I'm sorry, but I'm going to need to lie down. That was a lot, and I need to... rest after seeing an execution for the first time."

CHAPTER SEVEN

Unexpected Conversations

After several weeks of double shifts, Anca looked at Marin. "I'm going camping with some friends outside the inner wall, just off the main road. Would you like to join us?"

Marin looked at her friend, beginning to smile. A camping trip would be nice, especially in getting out of the city for a few days. She continued to roll bandages. "Who else is going?"

"A couple of the other nurses, the two who usually go on house calls, and their sisters. I didn't want anything too large, as that makes people nervous," Anca said. She shifted. "Honestly, it makes me nervous. I'm not a huge fan of being around that many people."

She smiled at Marin and the older redhead grinned. "I would love to go. When?"

"Tomorrow after our shift. I know it's a little sudden, but we have most everything set up outside of food-"

"If we really need to, I'm sure we can hunt."

Anca rose an eyebrow and Marin shifted. "Haven't you ever hunted for dinner while camping?"

"I'm from Zanther, remember? We have shops, we don't need to hunt for dinner."

Marin shook her head. "We'd die if we were stuck in the woods, then."

"I'm not that useless!" Anca laughed and turned from their task. "Can you help me with a couple of the newcoming patients? Justine has us on rotation today."

The day moved by quickly, as did the next. Marin spent a considerable amount of time in prayer when she was home, especially as she was wrestling with bringing her Holy Text on the trip. It was dangerous, but there was a strange feeling that she would need it.

Marin waited for the other members of the camping trip beside the gates, her pack filled with a canteen, bedroll, a change of clothes, a day's worth of emergency rations and her Holy Texts. She had opted for a pair of rough spun pants and a tunic rather than her usual gowns and had braided her wild red hair back, held with the same type of leather cord that held her hunting knife at her hip. She hadn't been able to purchase a bow, but she had a length of twine that she knew would work well enough to string a makeshift bow once she found a springy enough piece of wood.

While she had laughed at Rolandus teaching her how to survive and make a bow if something went wrong, she appreciated it now.

Anca was the next to arrive, her hair in a ponytail and her boots up to her knees. She had a couple of cooking pans and a bedroll, but that was all Marin knew she had. Then were the other two healers and a sister for each. They had opted for pants as well, but they nervously shifted as they grew closer to the gate. Marin glanced at them. "Are you ready?"

"What happens if we run into a chitter?" one asked.

Anca looked at Marin, who gave a bit of a shrug. "If you can run faster than someone else, you'll be okay. I might not be the best with a bow, but I can at least shoot one. We'll be fine, though. The guards do a good job in patrolling."

Her words didn't seem to comfort anyone and Anca spoke up, "We aren't that far from the gates: if something happens, the guards will hear us."

"If you're sure..."

The little group left and began their hike into the forested section between the inner and outer walls. They chatted idly until Marin stopped at a bush, inspecting its berries. Anca peered over her shoulder. "What'd you find?"

"We have some of these where I'm from. We used them for bleeding, but I can't remember what they're called off the top of my head." Marin laughed softly. "It's been long enough that I'm surprised I remember what they look like." She carefully picked one of the ripened red fruits and rolled it in her palm. "We'd use two for post-labor bleeding in new mothers. If they were doing poorly, we'd do 4 but..." She trailed off, a sad smile playing on her lips. "We don't use them in Zanther, and I don't think Justine would be very open to using them."

"Well, we have better medicines there, anyway," one of the other healers said. She shifted, looking around. "Medicines that we don't have to look for, as they're made for us. Those work just fine."

Marin nodded slowly and stood, keeping ahold of the berry before she carefully passed it towards Anca. "All the same, knowing what it looks like is a good idea. The leaf is different enough from others you might see, so you don't need to worry about accidently getting nightshade or anything else poisonous."

Anca took the berry and studied it in silence as they walked. Eventually, they stopped at a clearing and looked around. Anca nodded. "This looks like a good place to set up camp."

"Who brought a tent?" Marin asked.

The group looked at one another, silently, before Anca asked, "Didn't you say you had one, Hally?"

Hally, the healer who had rebuked Marin, shook her head violently. "I don't know what you're talking about. We don't have tents."

"Then... we have no tent?" Marin asked, raising an eyebrow.

Anca sighed. "Well, I guess we can go back and get one, though the avatar of Solaris is lowering."

"I would rather go home and try again than be caught without a tent," Hally said. She shifted. "This wasn't very well planned."

Marin glanced at Anca, realized how close her friend was to tears, and took her hand to comfort her. "Things will work out. Look, we're by trees with low, full boughs. While it isn't perfect, they make good rain shields should the sky open, and there are enough sticks and such on the ground that we can build a wall around the space place under the tree. We didn't bring food either, did we?"

The group slowly answered with headshakes and Marin looked at Anca. "Have you ever shot a bow?"

"Once, but I was very little."

"Has anyone?"

Again, no one had.

Marin took a deep breath. "Well, our camping trip can go one of two ways. The first is that we give up and leave now, or we rough it. I'm not the most skilled in dealing with situations like this, but between my older brother and my fiancé-" one of the healers scoffed quietly and Marin glanced at her before she continued, "between the two of them, I can at least keep us dry and our stomachs full. We'll need to gather dry sticks for a fire, and everything else will make a wall around the dry spot under the tree. Can you guys start doing that while I look for a branch to make into a bow and some arrows?"

Anca nodded and hurried off, though the other four took their time. Then, they moved to the other side of the clearing and spoke quietly to one another as they gathered sticks. Marin looked for a suitable branch, aware of their eyes on her the entire time.

Instead of focusing on it, Marin began to whittle smaller, straight, sticks into arrows. Then, after she was pleased with them, she strung her makeshift bow and carefully pulled it back. It wasn't perfect, but it would do. "I'll be back in a little bit."

Anca lifted her head. "Do you want someone to go with you?"

Marin shifted, before she nodded. "That would be nice." She slung her pack over her shoulders and looked around at the clearing. "Should I start a fire before we go?"

"Might as well."

The fire didn't take long as Marin struck flint and steel together, courtesy of Anca, and the two set out into the woods to hunt.

The first two arrows Marin fired at squirrels missed, and her bushy-tailed prey ran off. She groaned as she fetched them, "Rolandus makes this look so easy."

"He's also done archery for how long?"

"I suppose you're right." Marin knocked her arrow again, aimed at a squirrel, and fired. The rodent ducked and ran further up a tree, making Marin sigh, "It'd be nice to have him around right about now. He took a lot of time to teach me how to hunt when we were kids, just before my Da died. I owe him a lot."

"So that's how you two met," Anca mused. She looked up from a berry bush she had been picking. "I was wondering. You don't really talk about him much."

"I don't want to lose focus on what I've been called to do," Marin answered quietly. She pulled another arrow and then paused. "Keeping busy keeps me from growing sad."

"You find comfort in HaMelech too, don't you?" The words made Marin freeze and she slowly looked at Anca. Her friend was still kneeling beside the bush, focusing on the plant rather than her, as she continued, "You and Catherine aren't like the others at the infirmary. You have more patience than most of us, and..." she trailed off, her shoulders sagging. "There's a weird sense of hope that you both have, regardless of what's happening. I mean, you're in Zanther, surrounded by inquisitors, but you haven't given up. Why?"

Marin swallowed and then slowly lowered her bow. She stepped towards Anca. "How long have you known?"

"It didn't take long. I figured a couple of weeks into you being here," Anca murmured. "I didn't want to bring it up anywhere so loud because I do really like you, and I'm confused and... Marin, they tell us that you heretics are here to force us from Solaris, and are monsters who are undermining us. You haven't done any of that, even when you and I were in private, or Catherine and I were alone. What they say can't be true."

Marin took another step. "No, it isn't true. None of the Kingsmen are trying to undermine anything, and we aren't trying to force people from Solaris. Our job is to tell people about HaMelech, the One True King, so they have a chance to know what true love and relationship looks like. There is no forcing, there is no threatening, there is no making you listen to me if you don't want to. It's entirely up to you what you decide to do, my only goal is to let you know that HaMelech loves you, and you do not need to prove to Him anything for Him to continue loving you."

Anca slowly looked at Marin, searching her face, before she began to cry. In an instant, Marin was beside her, her bow abandoned, and held her tightly. Anca clung to her, finally managing, "Solaris isn't there, Marin. People keep saying he is, but I know... I know he is absent. I tried to use my prayer beads and there has been nothing! In fact, the last time I used them I felt like they were hot to the touch and they burned me like acid... I don't know what to do, but I know that there is no true power in Solaris. What do I do? Who is HaMelech?"

For a moment, Marin was quiet. Then, she pulled away enough to wipe Anca's eyes. "HaMelech is the True King, who sent His only Son, the Dove, to our world in order to die in our places. All of us have turned from HaMelech; we are creatures of chaos and were separated at the beginning of time due to disobedience. HaMelech never intended for us to turn from Him, and so He had created a plan even before our dis-obedience to allow us back to Him. The Dove died in our steads, as the only payment for the wrong we do is death, and we are now extended grace through the acceptance of HaMelech within our hearts. The price has been paid, we are now free... but that is only if we recognize and return to the King of Kings."

"Why did He let us turn from Him? If he is the True King, why did He let us rebel?" Anca whispered. Her eyes were red from her sobbing, something that made Marin worried that others would come to see them.

She brushed hair from Anca's face, suddenly growing aware of the darkness swirling around them to choke Anca. Deep in the shadows, a large hulking figure was striding to them. Marin pulled Anca closer, realizing her friend was shaking, and whispered, "HaMelech is might-ier than the darkness... the darkness I know you can feel. He allowed us to rebel because He will not force us into His will. We are given a choice regardless of what He desires, and it is our choice to accept the forgiveness and grace that he offers through the Dove's sacrifice." As Marin spoke, she held Anca tighter. The figure in the shadows was picking up speed, its abyss of a maw open wide in a silent scream.

Anca continued to shake. "How is He different from Solaris? Solaris offers a new life at the end of death...."

"Solaris offers the idea of a life after death, HaMelech gives a real life after death. His children join His embrace, and they remain with Him rather than a cycle of death and life over and over again. HaMelech wants us to join Him, not to remain separated." Marin watched the figure as it came upon them, finally sheltering Anca in her arms as her friend began to sob again. Her tongue began to itch and she began to speak rapidly, as the demon hulked over them as though to consume them. Incomprehensible words rolled off her tongue, too quiet for Anca to hear, but the demon stopped. In an instant, it recoiled as though it had touched a hot stove, raised what may have been its hands to the sides of its head, and then raced back to where it came. As quickly as they had come, the words stopped as if a tap had been turned off. In her arms, Anca's sobs were beginning to die down. Marin whispered, "HaMelech is the True God, and He loves you dearly, Anca. He knows about you, He knows the pain..." she trailed off, allowing herself to loosen her tongue for the Breath of HaMelech to use, and then, as if someone else had created the sentence she was speaking, whispered, "He knows what it was like, watching your parents die. He knows the pain of seeing someone you love so dearly slip away and the fear of not knowing what will happen next. HaMelech knows what will happen next. He knew what would happen before you were even born, and He sent his Dove to die for you... the real you, Anca, not the you that you keep pretending to be."

Her friend clung to her and Marin clutched her tightly. "He wants you, Anca."

"What do I do? Will He really want me after I served Solaris?"

"Of course He does!" Marin whispered. She stroked Anca's hair, letting her friend relax in her arms. "Anca, He wants you more than you could ever imagine... He truly loves you, more so than I or anyone else can as He is love." Marin looked around them. "The next step, if you want to be with HaMelech, is to invite Him into your heart. He is always with you: you don't need any amber to speak to Him. Whisper to Him, speak to Him, talk to Him."

Anca stared at Marin before she whispered, "I'm scared. I don't know what I'm doing, and... and I don't want to mess up."

"You won't."

Anca swallowed before she closed her eyes. Marin held her as Anca whispered, "I... want You in my life. I want to... I want to have a hope in the future like Marin has, and... and I want to have something after I die. I don't understand everything, I don't understand why you would want me, but I want you."

"Do you believe that HaMelech has given His Dove to cover your wrongdoings, the sins you have committed?" Marin asked quietly.

Her friend nodded. "I do... it brings me peace. I haven't known peace since before my parents... Marin, I never told you that my parents died."

"I know, but HaMelech did." Marin smoothed Anca's hair down again. "HaMelech, thank you for being with us now. Thank you for loving us despite what we've done, and thank you for giving Anca the boldness to ask a question that she wouldn't normally ask. We are so grateful to have you as our Father and our friend, and we want nothing more than to live lives pleasing to you. Thank you for the sacrifice of your Son in our stead so we may live with you in eternity."

As Marin grew quiet, Anca whispered, "Thank you for letting me be Yours. Please... help me to know who You are, and help me to grow closer to You."

The two remained together, sitting quietly as Marin showed Anca her copy of the Holy Texts, before they returned to hunting. When they managed to make it to the camp, this time with four scrawny squirrels, they found the others huddled around a nearly dead fire. "There you are! Neither of you returned and we didn't think you would! What took so long? Is that all you found?"

Marin leaned her makeshift bow against a log and then scanned their campsite.

A makeshift shelter had been hastily constructed, but it was little more than a pile of sticks. The fire was nearly dead, no logs beside it, and the four other woman outside of Anca looked like birds that had got caught in a rainstorm.

"Hey! Pay attention, we asked you a question!" Hally snapped.

Marin looked at the woman and then the squirrels she had shot and gutted. Finally, she said, "It is all that we found, alongside some berries. Anca had picked a good campsite where we have enough food to forage for." She sat down, pulled out her hunting knife, and began to skin the squirrels. Gags filled the air and Marin, keeping her head down, whispered a prayer to HaMelech in thanks for the meat they had harvested. Then, after finishing the processing, she began to cook the squirrels in a pan.

"I'm not eating that," one of the other women said.

Marin looked at her, raising an eyebrow. "You'll be hungry in the morning if you don't. Hungry bodies don't perform well, especially if you deal with a chitter."

Panic flashed over the faces of the gathered group and they each, meekly, took a piece of the cooked squirrels and began to eat. That night, each of the healers laid down in the shoddily constructed hut to rest. Marin kept her hands folded on her stomach, staring at the sky, as she listened to the other healers whisper.

"She's such a barbarian... did you see the way she tore into that poor creature?"

"Honestly, I'm surprised Anca asked her on this trip."

"I just can't believe that Justine allows her near patients..."

Marin clenched her jaw, sat up, and then gathered her blanket.

From the mat beside her, Anca rubbed her eyes. "Marin, where are you going?"

"Somewhere quieter to sleep. The 'barbarian' likes her rest," Marin said. She shot a glare at the other four women who had grown silent, and then looked at Anca. "If you need me, I'll be elsewhere tonight."

"It's dangerous after nightfall," Anca protested softly.

Marin gathered the remainder of her pack. "Only for people who continue to talk while on the ground. As far as I know, chitters can't climb."

Little sounds of panic left her tormentors and Anca frowned. "Are you certain?" Marin nodded and her friend sighed, "Alright... we'll see you in the morning, I guess."

The redhead wasted no time in finding a sturdy tree to climb, found a couple of branches that made a nice enough perch, and then fell asleep.

When she awoke with a sunbeam across her face, Marin caught sight of the other campers below. They were poking at the dead fire, shivering amid the dew, and muttering to one another. Anca wasn't anywhere to be found, and Marin, after a moment, sighed and climbed down. The four women looked at her. "You're still here."

"Of course I'm still here," Marin answered. She crouched at the fire and began to strike the flint and steel together to light it. "Where's Anca?"

"Don't know. She left early to take a walk. Stepped on Lilli earlier," Hally said with a shrug.

Marin glanced at her and then towards the woods. "I hope she's alright. I'll look for her if we don't see her within the hour."

The other four women nodded slowly and Marin sat back on her heels to watch the flames slowly come to life. Finally, she said, "I know none of you really like me. Your whispers last night weren't the quietest, and I am aware of what you think of me. You were also very clear about what you think of Anca's planning." She continued to stare at the flames. "Anca is a good woman, and she is trying desperately to engage with you and everyone else she knows in a way that we can enjoy. I don't care if you want to talk badly about me, or if you want to mock my voice or upbringing, but Anca is off limits." The woman looked up at them. "I love her dearly, she is one of my closest friends, and if I need to defend her, I will. Is that clear?"

No one spoke. Finally, Hally squared herself. "And what exactly are you planning on doing? Making us eat more of your weird cooking?"

"Do I need to plan vengeance preemptively?" Marin returned, meeting her gaze. "I think it would be best that we avoid that topic."

"You don't know what you'd do."

Marin stood, wiped her hands off on her pants, and then paused. Standing over Hally was the same demon who had followed Anca, though this time it seemed to care less about Marin there. The redhead stared at it and then looked at Hally. "I know that I would hope that you learn what has made you so bitter, and that I would spend time praying that you perhaps reach a point in your life where you finally realize who you truly are rather than being cruel and judgmental to others."

She watched as Hally's face changed from smug, to confused, and then to angry as she stuttered, "You... you witch! How dare you say those things!" In a moment, Hally had launched herself from her seat and towards Marin, who merely stepped out of the way.

The other three around the fire didn't move as Hally lunged again, and Marin caught her wrists gently. She stared at the woman. "This isn't going to fix anything, Hally, and you know this-"

"May Solaris rebirth you as a curseborn!" Hally spat, "You horrid, monstrous, barbaric freak!"

Marin didn't release her until Anca came running from the woods. "What's happening?"

"I think we had a shred of understanding," Marin said softly, staring at Hally.

Hally wiped her face. "I'm going home. If you're going to invite a freak from beyond the woods, Anca, I'm not going to come with you!"

Anca looked around wildly between the others, tears beginning to fill her eye. "Marin isn't a freak! I don't know what happened, but I know that-"

"She's the closest thing to a witch aside from a heretic, Anca!" Hally snapped, "I should have refused the moment you mentioned her name."

"I can leave instead, Anca, if you'd like me to." Marin folded her hands in front of her as she looked at her friend. "You told me that you were excited about this trip with everyone, and I'm willing to go so you can enjoy more company than just my own."

Her friend shifted, glanced at Hally and the other three, and then looked at Marin. Finally, she murmured, "I would much rather spend my time with someone who doesn't talk poorly about others." She sighed. "Maybe we should all just go home."

"Good. Then we can get away from that redhaired beast," Hally said. She sneered, "You're disgusting, Marin."

Before Marin could say anything, Anca had clenched her fists and turned on Hally. The usually calm blonde was breathing heavily, her eyes narrow. "Hally, I've heard enough from you. Just get going and leave the rest of us to enjoy the day."

"You know-"

Hally didn't get any other words out before Anca punched her in the nose, her eyes angry and her knuckles white. "Stop talking about my friends like they're nothing more than animals. Marin is a good woman, and I will not let you talk poorly about her again."

The other woman scrambled back, holding her bleeding nose. "You... you hit me!"

"And I'll do more if I need to!" Anca snapped.

Marin took Anca's arm. "Leave her be- she didn't need you to hit her."

"She was saying-"

"I know, but I can deal with what she says." Marin looked at Hally, "Head back to town if you'd like. We'll finish this weekend whether you stay..." She trailed off and frowned, beginning to look around.

Hally began to complain and Marin shushed her, "Something's wrong."

"Yeah, your face!"

"Shut up!" Marin snapped, quietly reaching for her knife. "The birds stopped singing. They were singing before, and now they've stopped."

"It's just a bunch of birds." Anca looked around. "That isn't... Marin..." She stepped back and Marin slowly turned to follow her shaking finger.

The other women behind her gasped and hurried to their feet as Marin stared at the shadowy demon that loomed towards them. Rather than the dark ethereal figures Marin had been seeing, this one was very much a solid, lithe, rabbit-like monster who began to cackle.

Marin blinked at the chitter, backed up two steps, and then glanced at the others. "Run!"

Her companions tore off as soon as she spoke, leaving Marin and Lilli, Hally's sister who seemed to be frozen in fear. Marin grabbed the other woman's arm, nearly dragging her behind her as she fled. She grabbed her pack from where it rested by a tree. The chitter laughed behind them, its paws tearing up the ground as it gained on them. In an instant, Lilli screamed.

Marin turned to see that it had leapt upon her back, its claws sink into one arm to stabilize itself. The sharpened bone it held, covered in bile, was raised to strike Lilli's exposed neck as it laughed and Marin, without any other thought, swung her bag. The chitter was thrown to the ground as it connected.

With renewed vigor, Lilli sprinted past Marin. Terror was wide in her eyes as she wailed, "Chitter!"

Ahead of her, Marin could hear the other woman screaming for help. Anca's voice was among them, giving Marin a semblance of comfort, before she slid under a log. The chitter leap over it and Marin turned just as it lunged again. The bone narrowly missed her and the chitter pivoted on the spot, ready to attack again, before a bolt sprouted from its chest.

With a thundering of hooves, a flaming sword cleaved the chitter in half. Marin was grabbed and pulled atop a horse, her chest heaving. Despite having been rescued by an inquisitor, Marin could only cling to the Solari who had saved her as she watched the chitter bubble and then dissolve into a thick, lingering smoke. By the time she realized what was happening, they had approached a small lookout tower and cabin where Anca, Hally, and the others were waiting.

"Marin? Marin, are you okay?!"

The inquisitor passed Marin down and Anca raced to her side, checking her over. "Did it bite you, did it hurt you?"

"No, I'm okay... the guard killed it before it could touch me," Marin whispered. She held tighter to her pack, feeling the weight of her Holy Texts against her stomach, and then looked at the inquisitor.

Now dismounted, the faceless guard stared at them before asking, "What summoned that thing?"

"I don't know," Marin said softly. She held tighter to Anca. "We were camping and nothing happened until this morning, when the group began to argue. I realized it had gotten quiet and then..."

"Then the chitter formed out of shadows," Anca finished, trembling.

"I see... You and your group, I want to see all of your prayer ambers-something called the chitter, and if there is a heretic amongst you then we will find her."

Marin and Anca pulled out their amber. Marin's crude amber ring shone in the light while Anca's necklace, though she hadn't been using it, was as polished as it ever was. The inquisitor inspected them and then glanced towards Marin's pack. "Hand me your bag."

"Yes, sir," Marin whispered.

Her heart began to pound as the inquisitor took it from her, watching as he began to search its contents. Hally and the others had hurried to them and were watching. Anca held onto Marin's hand as Hally said, "Thank goodness he was here. What did I tell you? Outsiders are not to be trusted- she's the reason that chitter showed up! If they hadn't let anyone walk through the gates into Zanther, we wouldn't be dealing with all of those disgusting newcomers."

The inquisitor paused, his hand halfway in Marin's bag, and looked towards Hally. Then, he silently handed the bag back to Marin and approached the others. "Show me your ambers."

They fumbled with their prayer stones and Hally straightened. "We have them, and they're in good condition... unlike hers."

"Show me your pack," the inquisitor returned, a cold aura coming from him. He snatched it from Hally, rummaging through it.

"You'll find everything a proper Zanther citizen will need... certainly a better bag to look through than an out-"

"I am from outside of the Zanther walls," the inquisitor interrupted, "and I suggest you refrain from commenting on outsiders again."

Hally's face drained as Anca held tighter to Marin. "Oh! I'm sorry, I didn't mean to offend you! I don't mean all outsiders, of course, just those who are like her, from Godrick's Rest!"

The inquisitor's grip grew tighter on the pack. "People like me, then?" He looked towards Marin. "You are from Godrick's Rest?" Marin nodded and he asked, "How is Leticia?"

"Leticia... You mean Grandma Letty?" Marin asked, blinking. The inquisitor didn't answer and Marin shifted. "I'm sorry, she didn't really go by Leticia while I was living with her. She's doing well: she has a beautiful garden that she is tending to. Last I saw her, there was no snow on the ground and she had plants growing despite the weather."

Her answer seemed to satisfy him and he turned to Hally. "State your name, little girl."

"H-Hally Tippington."

"One of the healers."

Hally nodded and the inquisitor shoved her pack into her arms. He asked each of the group their name before he paused at Lilli. "You were injured." Lilli's face went white as the inquisitor grabbed her arm and inspected it. Marin could see thin whisps of smoke coming from the wound, the only reassurance that it was healing, before the inquisitor looked at Lilli. "This is minor, you are fortunate. Wash it and keep it exposed to Solaris' light until the skin blisters. One of my men will check on you tomorrow to make sure it has not progressed." Lilli nodded and the inquisitor looked at Anca. "Is your sister still working?"

"Yes, sir." Anca held slightly tighter to Marin's arm. "Currently, she's spending time working and serving in the temple."

"She's a good girl. Very devoted." The inquisitor mounted his horse and turned it in a circle. "You are to return to Zanther proper as there is a chitter threat in these woods. As none of you were bitten, we will not need to cull. Should any of you begin to exhibit signs of the madness, inform a guard immediately: Solaris' mercy is greater than a life of madness." Marin nodded and turned before the inquisitor cleared his throat, "Miss Lott."

Her name made her freeze, especially as she became aware of how much the inquisitor knew without asking. "Yes, sir?"

"Give Grandma Letty my regards if you return. Us outsiders need to stick together, especially when Zanther citizens tend to look down on us." The inquisitor nodded to her and Marin slowly smiled.

"Thank you, really."

With that, the small group of healers hurried to the main road. Lilli tried to walk beside her sister and Hally shied away, making Marin approach her. She gently stopped Lilli. "Here, this will begin to help the healing, too. It's not much, but the petals will soothe whatever the venom causes."

"You're a witch, get away from my sister!" Hally snapped, pushing Marin back suddenly.

Marin opened her mouth to argue before Lilli said, "Thank you... for this, and saving me. I'm sorry I was so rude to you. You aren't... you aren't horrible at all. Just... different." She paused for a moment before she hugged Marin and then took the petals. "Do I eat them or..."

"Eat them for now, and I can give you more to make tea." Marin said, giving her a little smile. The group remained silent as they approached the city and then went their separate ways.

CHAPTER EIGHT

Advice

Over the next several weeks, Anca had blossomed in her faith as she asked whispered questions. Eventually, she had even asked for a copy of the Holy Texts for herself. James was happy to oblige, and each day Marin found that her friend would have more questions and a greater desire to serve HaMelech than before. Her passion was bleeding into her daily life as well: Marin could see that her patience and gentleness with both patients and staff seemed to have grown twofold overnight.

She had taken the oath of a Dove healer, as well, and Marin had done her best to help her understand how to enter worship even during the most dismal of situations. Marin, too, could tell that her own faith was growing. While it was difficult to be away from Rolandus, especially as it had been so long, she found herself praying for him throughout the day. His letters were being delivered faithfully, and as he was replying she assumed that he was receiving hers without any issue.

Several months into her stay with Anca, Marin found an apartment close to where she attended worship. It was a good price and was just big enough for her needs. After a brief discussion with Anca, she moved her belongings, the several planted baskets of Valri root, and settled. Rolandus had included several additional prayers in his letters, writing back and forth about the sheep dogs and the recent chitter issues. His chittering madness was survivable, though he admitted that he missed seeing her face and knew he would feel better if she was home. Still, he told her to remain where HaMelech had called her and that they would see each other again.

Despite not living with Anca any longer, Marin found herself chatting with the younger woman many, many times through the day. Eventually, Anca entered the infirmary with a dreamy sort of look on her face. "I met someone."

"Oh?"

"His name is Flick. We didn't talk much, but he was tall, and had beautiful dark eyes, and dark hair... there's something about the way that he carried himself and spoke to me... Oh! And he touched my hand. I mean, it wasn't romantic, since he was helping me stand, but still! He was kind and worried about me and..." she trailed off, beginning to blush, "I'm sorry, I know I'm rambling but... I've never been so excited to meet someone before!"

Marin glanced at Catherine, who smiled and shook her head. Then she looked at Anca. "Did you want to talk to him again?"

"I mean... I'd like to get to know him. He was rather attractive, and I'd like to at least see him again. I don't know if anything will come of it, but..."

"But you're not against the potential?" Marin asked.

Anca blushed and tucked her hair behind her ears. "Not really. I... think I like the idea of seeing him again if I can find him... I didn't tell him how to find me!"

"Oh, Anca... I'm sure you'll find him again. Zanther is a big city, but some things are meant to be. Just protect your heart," Catherine said. "You don't know what he believes."

"I know," Anca murmured. She paused, "I feel like Ha... I am supposed to get to know him, though, as though something has guided me to him." She glanced at Catherine and Marin. "It's crazy, isn't it?"

Marin watched her friend. "Anca, sometimes confirmation is all it takes. Spend time in prayer, and see what you discern. Guard your heart, guard your thoughts, but don't live in fear."

When Marin walked Anca home, chatting about their day and the young man Anca had met, they found Adriata waiting for them. The taller blonde had her arms crossed, a scowl across her face. "Anca, you have some explaining to do."

"What? I've been at work all day, and I haven't taken any of your clothes in months. Marin, why don't you stay for dinner? Then, for whatever it was that I've done, there is a witness." Anca put her bag down and Marin slowly undid her hat. "What did I do?"

"Two young men came to the brothel looking for you."

Anca's cheeks turned bright red. "Oh!"

"Uh huh... who were they?"

"I... I assume one of them was the young man I met today. I don't know who the other would be," Anca said, rubbing the back of her neck.

Marin cleared her throat, "Adriata, I've been with Anca since she arrived at the infirmary. No one stopped to see her there, I'm assuming it was likely a case of misdirection." She hung her hat on the hook, ignoring Adriata's glare. "Justine is very firm in not allowing outside visitors."

"Regardless, you need to avoid those sorts. Men are nothing but trouble, Anca."

After Adriata's complaints about men, Marin and Anca retired to the parlor. Once they were certain that Adriata had fallen asleep after dinner, they met together and Anca pulled out her copy of the Holy Texts. Then, they began to read together as Marin spoke, "When you see this young man again, you need to be certain that he does not lead you from HaMelech. Love is patient and kind, and it doesn't boast. This relationship you are hoping for must be built on trust and have an element of faith. When Rolandus... when Rolandus and I decided to become engaged, it was a promise before HaMelech and an invitation for Him to be ever present in our relationship. Something that we did, as we were both Kingsmen, was pray together. There was nothing more beautiful than... than being able to pray together and before the Lord in such a trusting and vulnerable manner."

A week later, after Marin had finished readying her apron for work, Anca nearly knocked her off of her feet when she opened the door. "Marin! Marin, guess what!!"

"What?"

"I met him again, and he walked me home!"

"Flick?"

"Yes, and he wants to meet again!" Anca helped Marin pick up the fallen produce, a look of love-sickness on her face. "I like meeting with him. He's clever, and sweet, and gentle... I like him, and I want to get to know him better."

Marin received daily reports from Anca over four months, listening to her younger friend gush over Flick and the conversations they had. Anca was late to work one morning, making Marin glance at Catherine with a frown. Finally, two hours late, Anca raced in.

"Where were you? Are you okay?" Marin asked.

"I... was with Flick last night."

Marin glanced at her, frowning. "Doing what?"

"... he has two children." Anca sat down, trying not to cry, "He has two children and his daughter, Drop... she's ill. I don't know if she'll make it through the night tonight."

"Oh, Anca... I'm so sorry." Marin crouched beside her, a hand on her shoulder, "Is there anything we can do for her?"

"Only an act of HaMelech can help her," Anca whispered. "He told me that he had many, many doctors but none of them.." She began to sob into Marin's shoulder, prompting the other woman to hold her close.

Eventually, she pulled away and wiped her eyes. Marin shifted. "Speak with HaMelech. He can do mighty things... healing is one of those."

"Will... you pray with me, please?"

"After work, my friend, as to keep prying ears from hearing..."

"No, now," Anca breathed. "Please. She needs it now."

Marin nodded, holding Anca close, and dipped her head. "HaMelech, You are a good Father and a patient healer. You know what ails our bodies, what ills we may have, and the weakness that our bones carry. Today, we kneel before You as children who know that our abilities are limited but Yours are mighty. Please, rest Your hand on Drop as she sleeps this evening. Bring healing to her body, bring peace to her father, and show Anca and Flick your power. We thank You for the mighty moves You are making in their lives, and all that You are going to do. You alone have the power to change fates and lives, and we thank you for doing so even in this city."

Anca was unable to speak, sobbing and shuddering in Marin's arms, before she whispered, "Please, be with them..."

It wasn't until Anca returned from lunch two days later that Marin received good news. The night prior, Drop's fever broke and she was on the mend.

Life continued this way over several months. They were preparing for Annabell's sixth birthday, a quiet gathering of just family and Marin. She had protested at first, not wanting to intrude, but Catherine insisted.

"She loves you as much as she loves us. You are family."

It was the next day, however, that Catherine entered the infirmary quieter than usual. Marin sat down the herbs she was preparing, suddenly feeling the room go cold. She blinked, willing the Breath of HaMelech to allow her to see what may be troubling Catherine, and nearly dropped the remainder of what was in her hands. The shadows that usually fled from Catherine were pressing against her, swirling in an attempt to choke out the light that shone from her. Marin stared at her friend. "Catherine-"

"I will tell you later, Marin," Catherine murmured. She began to empty her apron pockets, placed a little pouch on the table, and then hung her head. In an instant, Marin could see the woman's age and distress. Tears had started to streak down Catherine's cheeks, and she finally took a breath before she wiped her eyes. "Simply trouble with a patient, is all. I need to let Justine know how my house call went, and then I will speak to you."

Marin nodded silently and watched her friend slip off. Anca, from across the room, frowned and watched her go as well.

Outside the window, Marin caught sight of the white armor of an inquisitor. Her heart sank. Was Catherine found out?

When her friend returned, she quietly stood beside Marin to put her tools away. As she did so, she whispered, "I've been tending to High Inquisitor Treatis."

"I didn't think you were anymore... you said he was ill-"

"And it has grown worse. He's dying, and I have been selected to tend to him until his death," Catherine said softly. She paused, hung her head, and then breathed, "He knows."

Marin stared at her, finally asking, "He knows he's dying or... that..."

"He has guards posted throughout the city to keep watch for my family. He said that I am not to leave, else I've decided death," Catherine whispered. She looked at Marin, tears slowly running down her face. "I don't know how long we have until he decides to order my arrest. He is trying to make me turn from HaMelech."

She looked back at her task and Marin stared, unsure what to say. Finally, she asked, "Maybe he will die before he says anything?"

"Marin."

"I know it's a morbid thought, but if he did-"

"No, that isn't how this works," Catherine interrupted quietly. She looked around and then whispered, "Treatis will tell the others, and I will be executed regardless. I have been given a duty to see to his health until the end of my life, or his, and I will do so. Until the arrest is made, life is to move as it does." She stared at Marin, her eyes growing soft as she whispered, "I tell you because I know that you play a part in my story, Marin. I don't want you to worry about this: HaMelech knows the future, and it does us no good to worry about it until it comes. HaMelech brought you to Zanther and to my side for a reason, and I know that it is only fair for you to know the part you may play."

Marin stared at her, slowly nodding, and turned back to her work. "Are you going to tell Anca?"

"I will, but now is not the time."

"And... Annabell's birthday? Are you planning on celebrating it still?"

"We are, and if you want to come you are still welcome."

The woman nodded, and they fell silent again. She remained in silent prayer that day, wrestling with why HaMelech was allowing something like this to potentially happen and why Treatis was so evil in his ways. She didn't speak much to anyone, instead focusing on her quiet internal dialogue. That night, she wrote to Rolandus to tell him about this. She also asked him for any suggestions on what to do.

His response came several weeks later. Marin opened the parcel to find that he had worked on a present for Annabell since her last letter as well as his answer.

As always, his patience and understanding of the world shone through. Marin sighed as he reminded her of how the broken world caused fractures in people, and that HaMelech will be the one who ultimately fixed the problem. Afterall, vengeance and justice was His. Marin fell asleep with the letter to her chest.

The next day, the birthday dinner was had. Annabell sat at the head of the table in a new pink dress, her hair pulled up as she beamed. Catherine's small pie was cooling beside the fire, steaming from within the cast iron pot, which made Catherine announce, "It's time for presents, and then we can eat dessert!"

The first gift, from a couple of other children, was a pouch of dried fruits. Annabell squealed when she saw it, but it was forgotten as she opened her parent's present. It was a beautifully made dress, with small flowers embroidered on it. Annabell grinned at her mother and then hugged her father before she paused. The last present was from Marin, no bigger than her palm.

"Happy birthday, Annabell," Marin beamed.

The younger redhead grinned up at her before she tore open the small gift. Inside was the little wooden sheepdog that Rolandus had painstakingly carved for her, a special present that he was more than happy to include. Anabell stared at it, her eyes wide. "It's a sheepdog! Thank you Marin, thank you!"

Marin laughed and hugged the girl, glancing at Catherine. "Rolandus worked on it for her- I wrote to him several months ago to tell him how much she had enjoyed those stories and... well... he wanted to help me with her gift."

Catherine smiled from where she leaned against James. "I think it was an excellent idea. That's remarkable crafting, too. I'm envious of your future children!"

Marin smiled slightly at her friend and then turned to Anabell. "What do you want to name him?"

"Shep!"

The small family began to chat idly before Marin stopped. "Catherine, I saw someone pass past the window— it's later than usual for visitors, isn't it?"

"It is, and I don't know who would be coming by..."

As though to answer their question, a pounding on the door resounded through the house. "Catherine Conroy! Under the power of the High Inquisitor Treatis, you and your family are under arrest!"

James shot upright as the pounding continued. "Get Marin out of here, Catherine! Anabell, get your things..."

"James, my love, they know we have a child," Catherine said quietly.

Marin stared at them. "They're going to execute you."

"And they'll execute you as well if they find you," Catherine whispered. "At very least, we can hide you. James, distract them until I return." She took Marin's hands and held them tightly for a moment, before she hurried her friend deeper into the house. There, she opened a panel in the wall and lightly pushed Marin inside. "Stay quiet- they don't know you're here. Whatever happens, I know HaMelech's will is good. Right now, it's my job to make sure that you can make it out of our home in one piece-"

Her words were cut short by the splittering of wood and shouts emanating from the parlor. Towards the kitchen, a second voice demanded that James and Catherine show themselves. Catherine whipped away from the door and shut it quickly, abandoning Marin in darkness.

From where Marin was, she could hear people beginning to crash through the home: Catherine's voice rose above the din as Annabell began to cry and, after James began to speak, the sound of flesh striking flesh made Catherine scream. Marin managed to open the door slightly before something heavy fell against it and pushed her back, blocking the slit of light and brief glance of Catherine struggling against two inquisitors from sight.

In a matter of moments, it was silent.

Marin swallowed, trying to hear anything from beyond the door, before she tried to push it open again. The barricade on the other side moved only slightly before talking filled the air and Marin stopped, her heart pounding in her ears.

"They have no use for their junk anymore," one man said. "Might as well take what's useful in the name of the High Inquisitors and leave the rest to looters."

"It's a shame they forbade us from taking much for ourselves…"

"Shut it, would you, and start moving things."

A horrid crashing made the speakers laugh and Marin flinched, looking around wildly. It sounded like they were breaking dishes, laughing as they did so, before the noises eventually faded. Marin began to struggle with the door again before the voices returned and, with nothing else to do, she sunk to the ground.

She didn't dare make a sound, though she eventually began to pray, "HaMelech, please… please help me from this, help the Conroys… Please, do something, move your mighty hand. Help your children. I'm scared, I'm so very scared and-" She jumped as furniture outside her hiding place splintered and more laughter resounded. Marin shuddered. "Please, HaMelech, protect me…"

By the time the looters were gone, Marin had worn herself out. She was cold, her legs were stiff, and she was beginning to grow hungry. Once more she pushed against the door only to find that she could get no more than a hand out and, even then, was unable to find what had blocked her escape.

Without anything else to do, she made herself fall asleep.

When she woke the next day, Marin managed to push the door enough to see that the looters had destroyed wherever she could see from the slit in the door. The other thing she saw was a curious looking Zanther pigeon pecking around the ruined furniture. It paused, looked at her with giant eyes, and then went back to what it was doing.

Again, Marin went back to prayer.

When Marin next awoke, she could hear the sounds of flapping and hopping within the mess on the other side of the door. She peered through the slit and then jumped back, hitting her head, as the strange pigeon creature suddenly appeared before her. In its beak was a small scrap of bread that it had found. It cocked its head, dropped the bread, and hopped out of view. Marin looked at the bread. It seemed stale, but as her stomach groaned with hunger, she began to eat it. "Thank you, HaMelech…"

When she was little, she always thought the story of a man beneath a tree being fed by crows was strange. Now, as the head of another Zanther pigeon poked into her cubby with more bread, Marin was exceedingly grateful to HaMelech for His provisions.

She wasn't sure how long she remained in the cubby, though she knew that her body ached and her stomach, while not empty, burned with hunger. She fell asleep quicker each time she closed her eyes and, finally, she knew that if she fell asleep again there was no promise that she'd wake again.

Looters came through the house every so often, leaving the door open and destroying what was yet intact. Marin stayed pressed against the wall, unsure of whether to call for help or to fear being found. Eventually, Marin lost track of even the times that she fell asleep. As she ate a piece of bread offered by a Zanther pigeon, doing her best to keep her eyes open, she heard someone enter the house. This time, though, the individual didn't move furniture around. As far as Marin could tell, they simply sat in the middle of the room and began to sob.

It was a familiar sound, though it took Marin a moment to recognize it. When she did, Marin struggled to the door in an attempt to look out.

"Anca?"

Her friend was sitting amongst the rubble, tears streaming down her face. As she heard Marin's voice, she lifted her head and looked around. "Marin?"

"Anca, I'm over here!"

Anca stumbled to her feet and hurried towards where Marin was kept. She struggled for a moment, crying, "I thought you were dead! You didn't come to work, and then Catherine... Marin, Catherine was executed with her family. They're all dead and... and..." The door swung open and Marin collapsed into Anca's arms. There, she clung to the younger woman and began to cry as well.

What was left of the Conroy's home was in shambles. People had broken furniture, stolen the precious dishes that Catherine had so carefully tended, and destroyed the windows. Marin lifted her head to scan the ruins before her eyes landed on a small figurine that had somehow been untouched during the entire ordeal. She pulled away from Anca to brush rubble from the wooden sheepdog that Annabell had received just before their capture. Marin turned it over in her hand, tears falling down her face faster now, before she held it close to her heart and sobbed.

Once they had grieved, Anca helped her stand and they slowly walked from the house to where Marin had been staying. Fortunately, her home had yet to be ransacked but that did little to encourage her as she sunk to the ground beside the bed. As Anca slipped out to prepare her something to eat, Marin began to cry once more.

She wanted to return to Apple Ridge, where she could cling to Rolandus as she mourned. She wanted to leave Zanther, never to return, and to be safe with her family... not here.

"Why?!" She finally asked, sucking in a breath. "Why are you letting this happen to good people... Your people?! Why are you letting them kill us in the name of their sick god, while we can only accept our fates?

Why are you so mighty, and yet we are trembling before the Solari and all they do? WHY?!"

Her question hung in the air and she held onto herself, crying harder, before she whispered, "Why are you allowing your children to suffer at the hands of our enemies?"

She sobbed for several minutes. Finally, Marin closed her eyes and whispered, "I... trust You as this continues. I don't know why you let this happen... but I know that you are good and will use this to further your glory. You will work all things for good for those who love You, and I know that You will not break that promise. Thank you... Thank you for being faithful and for working things out for our good. Thank you for loving us when the world does not love us, and thank you for staying by our sides even during this dark time."

Anca sat beside her, helped her to eat some broth, and then combed the tangles from her hair. All Marin could do was whisper in her prayer tongue that HaMelech would move.

It took two days before Marin was strong enough to return to the infirmary, at which point Justine scolded her heavily for missing nearly a week's work. After a pathetic attempt at trying to explain and then nearly fainting as she stood up too quickly, she was instructed to return home and rest until she was able to stand without collapsing.

While she did rest, Marin found that Anca had taken it upon herself to tend to her. She woke several times to find that Anca had stopped by with some stew for her, that her clothes were freshly washed, or that Anca had carefully collected her mail for her to read.

Rolandus had written several letters, all of which arrived at the same time. They were worried about Marin, asking if she was safe, and giving updates about Apple Ridge. Olare was returning to Bleak Hollow and he was remaining, the sheepdogs had whelped again, and he had taken up all of the archery training. It seemed like Rolandus had taken over when Olare was gone, and Marin was extremely proud.

She quietly read them and placed them in her journal for safe-keeping. Then, she went about her business as usual. Neither she nor Anca talked about what happened, nor did they speak to anyone else about it. Instead, they simply tried to live their lives as though nothing changed.

Marin knew it wasn't healthy, but it was a coping mechanism. She spent time in prayer trying to come to terms with it, but the only thing that came was a soft whisper that her friends were no longer in pain and were instead rewarded with HaMelech's loving embrace for eternity.

Before she knew it, the Long Night had come again. Anca sat on the edge of her bed, watching her quietly. "Have you gone with any of the Knights before?"

Marin paused in her writing. "No. Last year, I remained in one of our churches to help those who were harmed by the chitters. I've been invited to help with the Knights, but my brother wouldn't let me... and I know Rolandus wouldn't let me either."

Anca nodded to herself and then said, "I'm nervous. What if I don't do enough?"

"You're doing more than most, and that is enough." Marin turned to face the other woman, offering a smile. "You've always done enough, Anca, as you've continued to follow HaMelech obediently. There is nothing more than you can do as you're already saved by grace. Now it's allowing yourself to become more like Him. We will never be able to do enough, only He can make a way for us to be 'enough'... and you are, as you are saved by Him."

They remained together for several hours before Marin slipped away first, going to one of the worship locations of the underground church. There, she spent several minutes brewing hot tea, getting together herbs and tinctures that she had prepared, and then sat to meditate. She knew that, outside, the sun had just risen and then had vanished.

The first chitter howl proved this, and Marin turned her eyes towards the ceiling. "HaMelech, help your children."

Before she knew it, Marin had patients of all walks of life in her little infirmary. Mothers, children, elders: none had been spared by the chitters. She flitted from person to person, holding their hands and resting her hand on their foreheads, as she prayed over them or offered them tea. Her store of herbs was growing low long before the night ended, though it helped.

Two other Dove healers joined her through the darkness, taking shifts and praying for protection over those in their care. Marin remained where she was until the sun rose again, after they offered hushed words of praise to HaMelech as He had defeated the Black Dragon once more, and then slipped home.

She wasn't alone for long before Anca came storming in, her blue eyes wide with fury and her hair falling from its place.

"I'm going to kill him!" Anca fumed, throwing her hat onto Marin's bed. "I'm going to kill him, and I'm going to kill him again when he stands before HaMelech to face judgment!"

"Calm down and tell me what happened!" Marin said, grabbing her friend's arms.

"He's an inquisitor! He's an inquisitor, and he killed Terius! He was going to kill me, too, and then realized it was me! I'm... I'm..." Anca trailed off. "I can't believe he lied to me."

Marin stared at her, trying to wrap her head around what Anca was going on about before she stopped. "Flick?"

"He lied to me! I trusted him, Marin!" Anca pulled away and then sat down, staring at the ground. "I was so stupid... I took him to our worship, he's met other Kingsmen and he's an inquisitor."

The words made Marin freeze, and, after a moment, she whispered, "You need to go. I'll give you a letter to take to Apple Ridge... Blackrock, even. You and everyone else who was with your group last night need to leave."

"I've told him about you, though!"

The redhead shook her head. "I'll be okay. It isn't my time to leave Zanther, regardless of if I want to go. HaMelech has something in my future, and I know that I need to remain here until then... but I will enter a safehouse until I know my next steps." She smiled at Anca, whose face had gone pale. "It's going to be okay, my friend."

Anca stared at her and then nodded before she hugged Marin tightly. Marin closed her eyes, doing her best to keep from crying, before she whispered, "I love you Anca. Head to the nearest safehouse, I'll deliver the letter to you within the hour."

"Okay..."

Marin watched Anca hurry from her home before she pulled out a parchment and began to scrawl a letter out to Rolandus. Halfway through writing, she paused, staring at the note before sighing and resuming. Brief and to the point, she explained that Anca would require shelter due to the Inquisitors' activities. Careful to keep it vague, ensuring that anyone other than Rolandus would find nothing suspicious.

She then wrote a second letter, this time postmarking it to send to Apple Ridge. This one was a statement asking him to keep an eye on correspondence, as things were growing more difficult. While she knew that it'd be too late for Rolandus to do anything if she did stop sending letters, it brought her some sense of closure.

Holding the letter close, Marin closed her eyes. "HaMelech... let this letter reach them safely."

Pulling her cloak over her head, more to cover her vibrant red hair than anything else, Marin stepped outside to mail the letter. She placed it into the postbox as a familiar face came around the corner. While Marin hadn't attended any of his worship services, she recognized him as one of the HaMelech priests who had visited before. He locked eyes with her and then hurried over. "Marin... child, I have a message for Anca. I heard from the others that an inquisitor saw her and knows her name-"

"She's leaving town today. Who's it from?"

He fumbled with a parchment. "I don't know his name, he knows Anca-"

"Was it a man with black hair?"

"No, it was a raven cote."

Marin took the parchment from him, and then scanned it. "I'll get this to her. She's at one of the safehouses, she isn't returning home."

The priest nodded and then hurried away. Marin hurried to the safehouse after gathering a couple of things for Anca to take as well. All the while, her mind was spinning. Inquisitors didn't ever decide to be merciful- Flick apologizing and asking to speak to Anca was out of the ordinary. The letter had to be some sort of a trap, right? On the other hand, Marin had seen miracles. Perhaps this was one, where Flick's letter and apology was sincere. A semblance of peace filled her at that idea and she sighed, as she entered the safehouse.

Anca was pacing, though she stopped and glanced at Marin. "That was quick."

"I tried. Though... this will only complicate things for you, my friend." Marin handed her the two letters, beginning to wring her hands. "Flick is looking for you: I don't know what you'll want to do, but he seems like he could be earnest in apologizing."

Anca glanced at her and then read the letter, anger and then pain flashing through her face before she crumpled it. "I... I still need to go."

"Anca, at least pray about this," Marin said gently. "I know that you're angry, and quite honestly, I am as well, but... if he's serious, it's worth considering. You could visit him, at least tell him that you forgive him."

"I don't want to see him."

"Then pray to HaMelech about it- even if you don't see Flick and speak to him, we don't need to harbor this anger. It's not healthy, you know this," Marin said.

Her friend sighed and nodded. "Alright... though I'll be staying here until I go."

"Of course." Marin hugged her and then left.

CHAPTER NINE

Last Rites

Anca sent her a letter several days later, stating that she had for-given Flick and was going to speak to him. Marin did what she could while working at the infirmary as Anca was in hiding, though it was difficult as Justine questioned her.

The Solari healer stared Marin down, tapping her quill on her ledger. "And where was it you said Anca was?"

"She wasn't feeling well, so she was staying elsewhere the last few days," Marin replied. She raised an eyebrow, her hands folded in front of her. "Justine, you know she doesn't miss work often. The Long Night was hard this year, even for the most devout. I'm certain she's simply recovering from the stresses that it brings."

"Mhm... very well. Get to work and, if you hear from her, send her to me."

Marin dipped her head, returning to grinding herbs and tending to the injured.

When Anca did return to the infirmary, she had a healthy glow and a light in her eyes. After a brief conversation, Anca told her that she and

Flick had reconciled. Not only that, Anca shared the news that Flick had turned to HaMelech and renounced Solaris.

Marin's joy was short-lived as Justine approached. "Marin!"

"Yes?"

"I have an assignment for you, and you mustn't say a word. Is that understood?"

Marin nodded and Justine handed her a small pouch. "An inquisitor will escort you to the patient's home. Once there, you will do all you are asked and will leave only when dismissed. This is for him: it's a simple administering."

Again, the redhead nodded and then turned to find that an inquisitor, fully shrouded, was waiting for her. Her heart sunk and she took a breath. There were only a limited number of possibilities for who she would be seeing, but she was confident she knew who it was.

Unlike the times that Marin seen arrests, this inquisitor didn't touch her. They instead walked by her side, gesturing for her to enter doorways first, and led her across the city. They stopped before a large manor surrounded by dark hedges. Marin entered the courtyard first, her concern growing as she caught sight of the coat of arms above the door.

An ivory six-tusked boar.

It was the symbol that High Inquisitor Treatis wore when he felt well months ago. Catherine had once explained that it was the holy animal of Solaris; each tusk represented a deity in the pantheon, while the white boar was a symbol of power.

Marin approached the door and the inquisitor knocked.

A thin maid opened the door, curtsied, and stepped aside. Up a long staircase and down a narrow hall, Marin looked around at grand images of Solari nobles and their power status. She stopped at a large oak door, her breath catching.

Again, the inquisitor knocked, and the doors opened. This time, a man wearing a uniform akin to the inquisitor's armor answered. He looked at Marin. "Name?"

"Marin Lott. Miss Justine sent-"

"I'm aware of who sent you. Come in." He then glanced at the inquisitor. "Wait outside until she is sent from the room."

Amber adorned the walls and furniture, though they were dull in the weak candlelight. The blinds were closed and the curtains surrounding the Master bed were shut on all but the far side. A hacking cough filled the air as Marin was led to the resting place before the thin, aged, and dying High Inquisitor Treatis.

He rested against several pillows, his white dressing robe wrinkled, with sunken eyes. Where Marin could once see noble features he had grown gaunt, now a shadow of the man he once was. Thin silver hair had been pulled back while various amber stones were lying about him.

As his coughing fit finished, Treatis looked at Marin.

His gaze made her shrink, especially as the realization that he had last seen Catherine before her arrest filled her.

"Who are you?"

"This is Miss Lott, sent from the infirmary, High Inquisitor," the other man said. "She is here to aid you and assist your comfort."

Marin stepped forward. "I'm not sure if I can do much, I'm afraid. Miss Justine didn't explain how you are doing, only that I've medicine I can administer." She opened the little pouch of medicine and paused as she realized it was a vial and a syringe.

As she drew up the liquid into the syringe, she became ever aware that it was a concentrated dose of painkiller- three times as much as she was ever instructed to administer. With a sad realization, it dawned on her that the treatment was simply making the High Inquisitor comfortable as he died.

"Well?" Treatis questioned, coughing again.

Marin quietly prepped his arm and then gave him the injection. As she did, she watched his face. Within moments, it was as if everything faded away, replaced by relief flooding through him. His eyes opened, and he studied her with gratitude.

Despite his appearance, Marin knew that he was even more dangerous than she had assumed.

The man was silent as he sat up. After he regained his bearings, he looked at Marin again. "Sit. My eyesight is failing, and I want you to read to me from the papers."

Marin nodded and sunk into a seat. She lifted the papers and began to read them aloud, keeping a careful eye on him as he rested on the bed. Eventually, he interrupted her with a cough, "You must have worked with Catherine."

Marin looked at him, "I did. She was a dear friend of mine and showed me around the city when I first moved here."

"Where are you from?"

Marin slowly set the papers down. She took a breath, willing herself to give the lie that she had used for over a year and a half, before she said, "Apple Ridge. I did training in Godrick's Rest but grew up in Apple Ridge."

Treatis stared at her, his eyes narrowing slightly. He didn't say much for several minutes, though he did cough horribly, and then he asked, "Why did you agree to treat me?"

Once more, Marin was quiet. She watched him, aware of his tired eyes scanning her face. "It is my job to tend to the ill. While you may serve on the Council, you are still simply a patient who needs aid. The medicine I gave you is strong, strong enough that I know how poorly you are doing, and at the very least I can help make you comfortable while I serve you."

"Interesting." Treatis coughed and then gestured towards the door. "That will be enough for today, Miss Lott. I will send word when I need your services again."

He turned away from her and Marin, doing her best to remain calm, hurried from his room. She was escorted back to the infirmary where Anca was waiting for her. "Marin! You were gone for hours!"

"I know," Marin whispered. "Treatis is dying. I was sent to his home."

Her friend blinked at her and then hugged her. "HaMelech keep you... What are you going to do?"

"What He has called me to do. There's a reason I'm to do this, and I will remain obedient."

When Marin returned home, she found that Rolandus had sent her another letter- she assumed he had sent it by dove, though she wasn't sure if that was the case. She spent several hours curled beside the fire as she read his words over and over. It was comforting to know that they were doing well and that he was still thinking of her. Then, she wrote back to him and told him all that had happened.

The next few weeks flew by quickly, so quickly that Marin felt like she had no time to breathe. Between serving in the infirmary, tending to those ill with chittering sickness, and being sent to High Inquisitor Treatis once or twice a week, she was stretched thin. It was a saving grace that Rolandus was faithful in returning her writing, as she returned home to opened and resealed letters regularly.

Treatis was at least an easy patient. He would do the same thing each time Marin attended him, and very rarely did he speak to Marin after their first meeting. Towards the end of a two-month period, though, he was sitting up when Marin came. There were two inquisitors outside the oak doors and his righthand man, the thin man from before, was speaking to him as Marin entered. Treatis waved the man out.

"Shut the door behind you," the old man said, "I wish to be alone with the healer."

The man beside him raised an eyebrow before he stepped out and closed the heavy doors behind him.

Just as she did each week, though usually not alone, Marin sat beside Treatis' bed and lifted a book. "Where would you like me to start today?"

"By explaining why you have defied Solaris for so long, Miss Lott," Treatis replied.

Marin paused at his words, lifting her eyes from the book, and then said, "I'm sorry?"

Treatis sat up, heaving for breath. "Don't play coy: you are a Kingsman. Why do you defy Solaris as you do? What is it about the Usurper that makes you follow him?"

Out of the corner of her eye, Marin could see Treatis' sword leaning against a corner. It had been a while since he was able to use it, but that didn't matter as she saw the edges begin to glow red hot. She sat her book down, gazed at her lap, and sighed. Finally, she looked at Treatis. "I follow Him because I know that He loves me, and doesn't force me to fear Him."

The old man furrowed his brow, silent, and laid back. He closed his eyes, briefly, and Marin said, "I'm not the only Kingsman who's been here to heal you. Catherine was, too."

"She was a good woman, aside from her heretical practices. It was a shame, I wish she had decided to listen to me." Treatis sighed and shook his head. "She would have been saved, and Solaris would have blessed her in her next life. He does with all who follow him... though I know my time has come to leave this world forever."

Marin blinked, daring to whisper, "What had you asked Catherine?"

He didn't answer her for several moments. When he did, his fragility and age were more clear than Marin had ever seen. "If she had renounced your god, I would have pardoned her."

His answer hung in the air and Marin stared at him. His eyes had grown distant, nearly tear filled, and he quietly said, "There are some in this world who I would have given anything to help. Catherine... she tended to me well, and she was a gentle creature. I never had children of my own, but... she was the closest thing to a child I ever had. I loved her... and she refused the one gift I could give her."

Marin sat in silence, unsure what to say. She stared at the man before realizing that Treatis was growing angry, his hands shaking as he managed to sit upright again. "Why didn't Catherine take my pardon? Why did she refuse to bend a knee and give up the Usurper? She condemned her own family to death. I gave her a way out, but she refused."

Marin stared at the old man, her voice trembling less than she thought it would as she murmured, "... because Catherine knew that an eternity with HaMelech is better than a single day on Illeross following a demon as a king."

The High Inquisitor stared back at her, his cloudy eyes hard, and he lifted one gnarled finger. "You could be saved too, stubborn girl-"

"I have been. But it isn't you or Solaris who have saved me," Marin interrupted. She shifted, swallowed back a lump in her throat, and said, "I was saved by a God who gave His only Son, the Dove of HaMelech, to die in my stead and to pardon me of all my sins so that I may live with them in His embrace eternal. I know that I do not need to bow to a demon king, or to a man who believes that he has been given power... because you do not have power. The only thing you can do is to kill me, which would send me to my home and would hang over your head just as every deed you have done, great and small, does now. I have been saved, Treatis... have you?"

She remained where she was, though Marin was terrified that the High Inquisitor would throw his aged body from his bed in an attack. Instead, Treatis blinked at her and offered her a tired smile. "I will admit, it's refreshing to see someone so passionate about what they believe, even if they're wrong."

"You may say I'm wrong, but I would much rather die being wrong about HaMelech being real than to be wrong about Him never existing."

Treatis didn't argue as he settled back, giving a horrible cough that shook the bed he laid in. Marin stared at him before she lifted a kerchief and held it to his mouth. He hacked up several clots of blood, trembling as he grasped at her wrist in an attempt to give himself comfort, and Marin finally murmured, "Have some tea, it'll help your throat." Treatis slowly released her and she pressed his teacup to his lips. The shaking hadn't stopped, which made Marin hold the cup ever tighter as sadness filled her heart.

He was alone, with no one who knew him there to comfort him as he died. There was only fear, and pain, that surrounded him. As Marin watched him, she realized that the darkness was beginning to choke him. Dark ethereals swirled around him, sucking away what life he had. Without much thought, Marin took his hand, making him tense, and held it softly. "Regardless of what you've done, HaMelech hasn't closed the doors on you... and I pray that you may come to know Him despite this life you've led."

"Stupid, stubborn girl," Treatis rasped, "Headstrong and... and bold. At the very least I can thank you for making my final days comfortable. Please, give me something for the pain so I may slip away in peace."

"Catherine scared you, didn't she?" Marin asked quietly. He glared at her and she pulled the syringe from its pouch. "She told you the same things I did, and you aren't sure what may happen after you die."

Treatis' eyes narrowed and he coughed, "What I am afraid of does not concern you."

"No, it doesn't... but I know that you cared about what Catherine thought, and that you hope to maybe see her again." Marin watched him, realizing that he was beginning to cry. "I hope that you may be able to, but I know that is only a conversation that you may have with HaMelech." Marin administered the drugs as he looked away, holding his hand once more as relief flooded his face. He stared at her for a moment, some semblance of gratefulness in his eyes, before he closed them. Within a handful of moments, his chest stopped rising and his hand went limp.

She remained with Treatis' body, praying to HaMelech, before she covered his face with the bedlinen and started to the door. On the other side of the grand oak barriers stood the waiting party. Marin folded her hands before herself. "High Inquisitor Treatis is dead."

The inquisitors raced inside the room at the news, leaving Marin and the attendant in the hall. She knew it was to verify her words, even more so to be certain that she hadn't killed Treatis while alone. Eventually, they returned to the hallway and stood, stoically. Even though they said nothing, Marin could tell by the subtle shifting that they were agreeing with her words.

"So he is. Miss Lott, you are under arrest for practicing witchcraft and spreading heretical thoughts through Zanther. Your final moments with the late High Inquisitor Treatis have proven your guilt as even now we can see your unyielding faith in the Usurper. Come quietly, as you face your execution in the morning," the former attendant said softly. "He had his suspicions, and you confirmed them through your conversation with him."

Marin stared at him, a sad smile playing over her face. "I expected him to have told you, just as he did with Catherine."

The two inquisitors stepped forward, each taking Marin's arms. There was no fight as they led her from the High Inquisitor's home and down the streets towards the Grand Citadel. The moment that she was seen walking down the streets, people came out to boo and jeer in her direction. People spat on Marin, called her names, and threatened her as they watched her go. The inquisitors leading her down the road said nothing.

As they entered the citadel and then went below the floors into a dark, damp dungeon, Marin could hear crying and screaming. They stopped at the first set of cells where Marin was unceremoniously thrown to the ground.

She lifted her head as they walked away, surprised that they hadn't beaten her yet before she looked around. Around her were familiar faces of people she knew from her church group.

No more than two hours later the inquisitors returned. This time, they beat and abused each person in the cell- including Marin. As soon as they were done, they chained each to the wall and then left again. Marin sucked in a breath, trying to ignore the pain in her ribs, and closed her eyes.

Though they were well beneath the citadel, it didn't take long before Marin could smell smoke from a fire and hear bells tolling. She managed to fold her hands before herself and began to pray, her voice not even strong enough for her to hear, "Mighty King... please, accept my soul into Your hands and hold it. Let my death glorify You and show Your grace in my life... and help Rolandus... Rolandus..."

She trailed off, her eyes opening as she stared at the ground in front of her. Tears were beginning to streak down her face as she finally whispered, "Help Rolandus hold ever tighter to You as we wait to be together again. You love him more than we can ever comprehend, and I pray that You help him transition into this life without... me."

Marin fell asleep during her prayer, leaning against the stone wall as her head pounded and her wounds stung. Her rest was short-lived, though, as four Inquisitors entered the dungeon and began to force the others back. Two of them held whips, more as a threat than an active use, while the other two approached Marin.

"Get up," one of them said. "We have orders for you to move."

Marin coughed and staggered to her feet. The chains around her wrists ached more than before, and as she walked from her cell to an uncertain fate, all she could do was whisper, "HaMelech, hold me."

Those behind her cried out in pain as the whips began to crack. Some of the voices renounced HaMelech, others cried out louder for Him. Marin closed her eyes in an attempt to drown them out as they led her up the stairs, through the citadel, and across town toward a private keep marked with 2 ravens with arrows in their necks.

The crest of High Inquisitor Alastar.

Afterword

Thank you very much for reading Tales of Illeross: Gracefully Broken! This has been a labor of love that we've been excited to share. While the ending seems to be abrupt, there is good news! God, who we call HaMelech, works all things for the good of those who love Him (Romans 8:28), and we know that Marin very much loves Him. This ending has been left ambiguous to serve a couple of reasons: the first is to allow you to determine what might happen if you were in Marin's place. Would you continue to follow your diety even in the face of death? The other is to comment on the uncertainty of our lives outside of what we believe. As Christians, we know that there is a life after death for those who know the Lord- with Marin, the story doesn't state if she is rescued or if she is executed. If you are interested in the remainder of the story as we have written it, check out *Turning Point*, the continuation of Anca's faith and the happenings around Marin. In addition, if you're able, we would love if you could leave a review of this book on either Amazon or Goodreads.

The World of Illeross

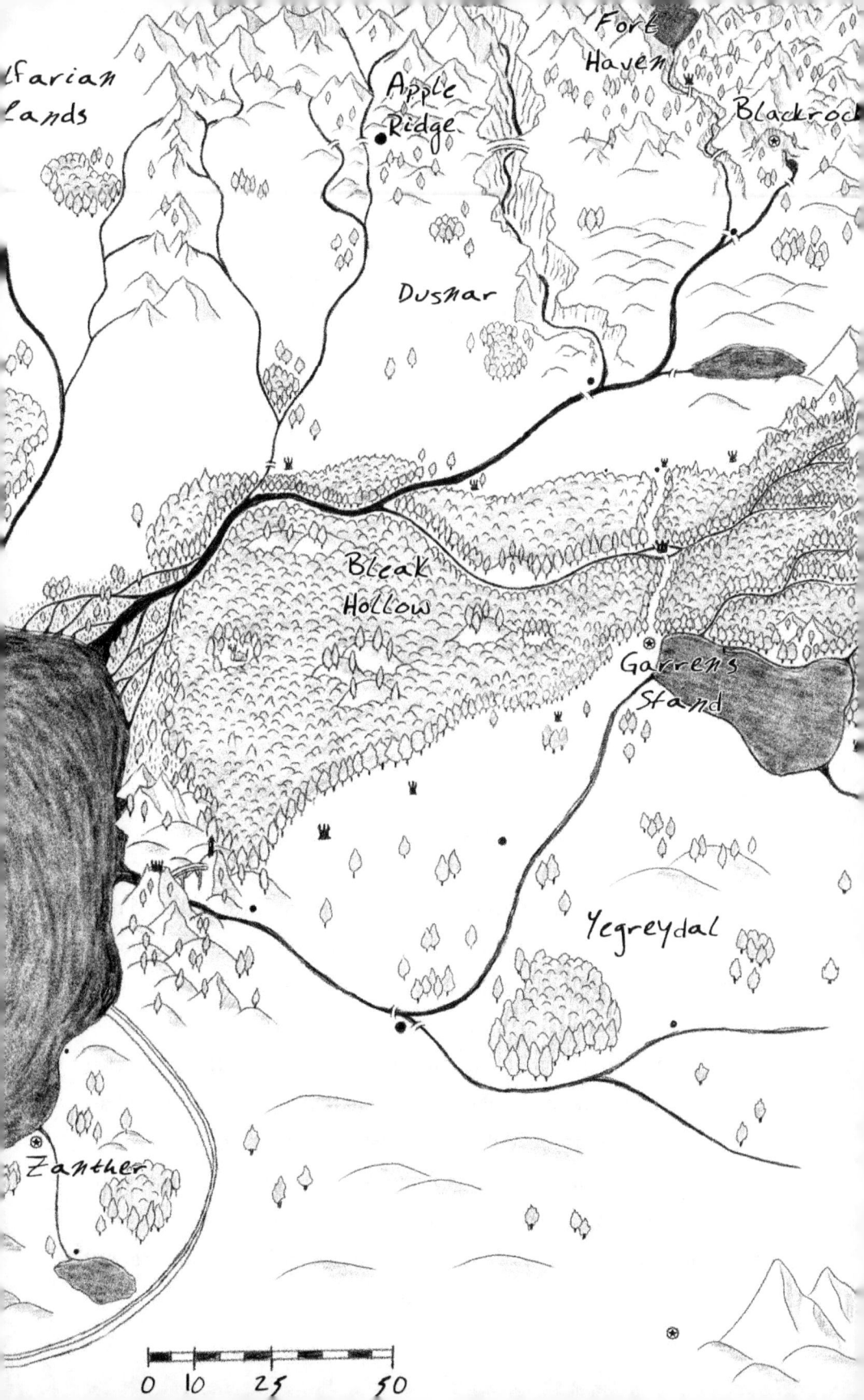

About the author

Ellie Lerum is a fantasy author and blogger whose stories blend redemptive hope, emotional depth, and a touch of whimsy. A devout Christian and mother of dragons (well, griffins... and two spirited little girls), she writes tales that wrestle with grief, healing, and courage through richly imagined worlds. Ellie draws inspiration from her faith, real-life loss, and the works of J.R.R. Tolkien to craft narratives that are both adventurous and deeply human. Whether writing or exploring Idaho with her family, she finds the greatest joy in connecting with readers who see themselves in the stories she tells.

Follow her on Facebook and Instagram @AuthorEllieLerum, or at aut horellielerum.com

Also by Ellie Lerum

The Cassy Series

Book 1: Phantom in the Dark
Book 2: Souls in the Ice
Book 3: Specter in the Shadows
Book 4: Wraith in the Light

Tales of Illeross

Turning Point
Gracefully Broken
A Mother's Prayer

Children Books

Animals of Illeross: An A-Z Alphabet